Dancing On Moonbeams

Jennie's Gifts Book 2

Dancing On Moonbeams

Jennie's Gifts Book 2

a novel by

LYNN THOMAS

Net Partners Publishing
2013 USA

Copyright

Dancing on Moonbeams
Jennie's Gifts Book 2

This is a work of fiction. Names, characters, places and incidents are either products of the author's imagination or used fictitiously. Any resemblance to actual persons, living or dead, business establishments, events or locales is entirely coincidental. All trademarks and brand names used in this book are the property of their respective owners.

Published by NetPartnersPublishing.com
Published in the United States of America
2014 Cover Design by: www.StunningBookCovers.com

Print ISBN#:0615895689

Jennie's Gifts Series

" ... a feel-good read in and of itself, but filled with spiritual wisdom that will open your heart and lift your soul. We need more books like Jennie's Gifts and more authors like Lynn Thomas." ~ Suzanne Giesemann, Hay House author of "Messages of Hope"

"Guess what I did yesterday? I read this Fabulous Jennie's Gifts Book 2. I absolutely LOVED it! Can really enjoy and identify with Jennie and her adventures. So much info given on so many different levels in each of her sessions with clients. Awesome! The personal touch is SPOT ON! Her interactions with Family is priceless. Hmmm, what could be next? I have a few more spoons!" ~ Joan Piper, mediumship instructor.

"I couldn't put the first book down and read it quickly. Went to bed and my other self wouldn't let the book go, so up I got and started underlining parts that were connecting to me... Meeting Lynn and feeling her energy when she walks into a room, brought me to an awareness that has been missing in my current life. Her books are enhancing this awareness, making me seek another level of understanding and spiritual growth. I am reading her book 2 much more slowly, and doing my spirit work, looking at my life and where I want to be. Thank you!" ~ Judy Greenwell

"Lynn Thomas accurately depicts the life of a medium and contributes greatly to mediumship by showing, with respect and understanding, that what we do is an act of love." ~ Janis Murphy, medium

"I really enjoyed the second book as I was now more familiar with the 'spirit world' and it made for an even more delightful read!" Sue McCloughy

Acknowledgements

With gratitude, I acknowledge my husband, family and friends for their loving encouragement and support. Heartfelt thanks to Angela P. Thomas in the creation of the original cover design. Jamey Thomas for her numerous proofreads. Joan Piper, for her instruction, guidance and inspiration; and to all who serve to enlighten and empower us on our journey. And a special thanks to the creative and loving Spirit in which this was written. And acknowledging you, Dear Reader, may this book inspire and entertain you!

Special Mention

Our dog, Max, passed away during the writing of this book. He was a cherished member of our family and his companionship, unconditional love and wonderful personality is greatly missed. We are most grateful for the time we had with our pup.

More about Max at: http://lynnthomas.info/max/

Dedication

With Love to
Jamey and Angela.

And as always, much Love
and thanks to my husband Tom.

CHAPTER ONE

January

THE MOONBEAMS HOVERED in space like lily pads floating on the surface of a pond. It's not the first time I've had this dream of skipping and dancing along the celestial pathway. I caught sight of the Earth below, and when I stopped to gaze down at the lovely planet, I felt a vibration in the filament. Something or someone had stepped on the path.

It was a man, and he was walking toward me along the illuminated threads. He was dressed in dark brown trousers and his white long sleeved shirt was tucked in at the waist. His hat was tilted forward, shadowing his face. As he neared me, he removed his hat, revealing friendly blue eyes.

"Hi, Jennie," he said.

"Who are you?" I asked.

"You'll remember soon," he said with a laugh, then whistled and shouted, "Jinx!"

A cat appeared on the bright strands of light and jumped up into his arms. "We'll see you later," the man said. He then donned his hat and walked away cradling the contented tabby, its tail flicking under his arm. He strolled several yards before they disappeared into the starlit mist.

Who the heck was that?

"You'll know soon enough," a voice said from behind me.

I turned around, and gazed up at a tall shimmering entity. "And who are you?"

"I am one of your guides, and you need to get going," he said, and pressed a fingertip to my forehead.

☼

My bedroom was dark as I opened my eyes. What woke me so early? I recalled a snippet of a dream, something to do with the moon? I grasped at it, but it slipped away.

Jake was sleeping soundly beside me, and drew me in with his magnetism. I snuggled up to him and was drifting back to sleep, when my spirit guide, Mica, said, "Wake up."

I sat up, rubbing the sleep from my eyes, as I silently asked, '*Where do I have to be so early?*'

"You need to get to your store."

My Sunflowers Shoppe is where I work as a professional medium. The store's located just off the main square in the small central Florida town of Del Vista.

"Get up!" Mica said.

I leapt from my bed and ran into the bathroom. I showered, towel dried and blew dry my hair in record time. As I stood at the mirror, slathering foundation on my face, the dream edged back into my mind. I stared at my reflection as I tried to recall it, but it was too disjointed.

"Hurry and leave now," Mica said.

I've learned to trust and rely on Mica's guidance, so I shouldn't waste another minute. But I was foggy minded this early in the morning, and stood in my closet staring at my clothes. A green and blue dress stood out, and I pulled it from the hangar and slipped it on.

Before leaving the room, I walked up to the bed and gazed down at Jake. He was still slumbering, and it took all of my will power to not climb back in bed and cuddle him.

"Go now, Jennie," Mica said.

I sighed, kissed Jake's cheek, and reluctantly left the room.

In the kitchen, I grabbed a breakfast bar, and wrote a note to Jake that I had to leave early for work.

As I drove toward town, I felt grateful that Jake was supportive of my profession, unlike my ex-husband, Ben Malone. And Ben's mother, Evonne, who never wanted me to marry her darling boy, continues to spread rumors about me, even after the divorce. Why can't she just leave me alone? And while Ben's not as vicious, he publicly mocks my career. I doubt I would have become a professional medium had I stayed married to him.

But despite our dreadful marriage, we had been blessed with two children. Our son, Nathan, lived in Portage Lakes, Ohio with his wife Bridgette and their daughter Emily, aged two. They were expecting their second child in a few months. Our daughter, Kate, lived less than an hour away from me with her children Lola, age four, and Evan, who is three.

The Sunflowers Shoppe came into view as I turned off Main Street and passed the town square. I pulled into a parking space and looked out at my store and the large potted geraniums under the windows.

As I stepped onto the sidewalk, the wind chimes rang out in the predawn breeze. I gazed up at them hanging above my door, and at my signage. I had chosen the sunflower for my store's name and logo, because it is a symbol of mediumship and of good luck.

I unlocked the door and stepped inside. It would be several hours before Megan, my assistant and store manager, arrived. I had hired her just days before our grand opening last fall. She has proven to be invaluable, has a pleasant personality, and is wise beyond her years. And she is well liked by our customers, who delight in the unusual items she stocks on our shelves. Thanks to word of mouth the store had become profitable, and requests for private readings have increased.

Still not knowing why I was summoned to work so early, I walked down the hallway to my office, and tossed my purse on my desk. The layout of the room had proven functional. My chair swiveled between my reading table and the roll top desk. The desk hid my computer and paperwork when I'm in session. Across the table from where I sit were two upholstered chairs for clients. Along the far wall, a couch offered extra seating, or a place for a quick nap.

And speaking of naps, the couch looked inviting. I stretched out on it, and as I was drifting to the edge of sleep, a loud ringing woke me. I glanced at my watch, it was only six o'clock. Who would be calling at this hour?

I walked over to the desk, and answered the phone. "Hello?"

"Hello, I'm looking for Jennie. Is she there?" a woman said.

"Yes, this is Jennie," I said.

"Oh, I'm so glad to reach you. My name is Caroline Werther. My cousin, Joyce Dillon, told me about you, and gave me your number."

"How can I help you?" I asked as I jotted myself a note to thank JD for all the referrals she sends my way.

"I'm in the hospital with my mother. She's been unconscious since yesterday. Her doctor says it won't be much longer."

"I'm sorry to hear that," I said.

"Yes, well, the reason I'm calling is that my mother had told me that, on his death bed, my father had promised to come for her when her time came. I mentioned this to JD, and she said you could tell me if my dad's spirit was here with her. Can you do that? Will you come here right away?"

'*Was this the reason I had been summoned to work so early?*' I silently asked my guides. My arms tingled, confirming it was.

"I'll come right over," I said.

"Oh, thank you," she said. "My husband, Keith, will meet you in the lobby and escort you to her room. Please hurry."

My gut tightened as I hung up the phone. I've never sat with anyone who was about to make their transition. '*What should I do?*' I asked.

"Trust," Mica said.

My guide's presence comforted me, I wasn't alone.

On my way out of the store, I stopped at Megan's desk and wrote her a note about where I'd be.

☼

As I drove to County General I recalled being a volunteer at a nursing home when I was about thirteen. At that time, I thought I wanted to be a nurse, and this offered an opportunity to try it out.

Mrs. Conley, the head nurse at the home, gave me my first assignment. The patient laid flat on her back, staring at the ceiling, unable to move or speak. As I observed her, I became overcome with empathy. When I leaned toward her, the room started spinning. The next thing I knew, I was waking up on a sofa in the nursing office.

"You passed out," Mrs. Conley said as she pulled the smelling salts away from my nose.

"I did?" I asked. My midsection hurt as I sat up. I rubbed it and asked, "Why does my stomach hurt so much?"

"You fell over the bedrail."

"On top of that woman?"

"Yes," she said.

"Oh, how awful!"

"Why did you pass out?"

I told Mrs. Conley how sorry I felt for the patient, and said, "The last thing I remember was the room spinning."

"You are not cut out for nursing, my Dear," she said.

She was right about that.

A week later, I dreamt of seeing the woman's spirit. I telephoned Mrs. Conley to ask about the patient, and she said, "She died during the night."

My experience at the nursing home made it obvious that I would not make a good nurse. But I had received my first confirmed prophetic dream. And I discovered the danger of becoming overly empathetic.

Over the years I have strived to be compassionate without being a sponge. Absorbing another's emotions has proven to be unhealthy.

CHAPTER TWO

AS I PULLED INTO a parking space at the hospital, one of my favorite songs finished playing. I found the music energizing, and pressed replay for another dose of the upbeat tune. After the last note played, I turned off the ignition and stepped from my vehicle.

I walked up the steps to the main entrance and entered the lobby. A tall, thin man was pacing the carpet there. His shirt was imprinted with a company logo, and from his paint splattered pants and work boots, I gathered he worked in construction. As I walked toward him, he stopped and looked at me.

"Are you Jennie?" he asked.

"Yes, I am," I said.

"I'm Keith. Follow me," he said and took off at a quick trot. I had to nearly run to keep up with his long stride. By the time I caught up with him at the elevator he was holding the door open for me.

"I hate the idea of Caroline's mother dying," he said as we ascended floors. "She and her mother are very close, and I fear how she's going to handle this."

Before I could respond, the doors opened and Keith exited, again at a quick pace. He took a right up ahead and as I rounded the corner, I nearly bumped into him.

"They're in there," he said as he stood in front of a closed door.

"Aren't you going in?" I asked.

"No, I've already said goodbye to Wanda. I can't sit in that room waiting for her to die. If Caroline needs me I'll be over there," he said as he pointed at the waiting room across the hall. It was stocked with puzzles, magazines and a television, offering plenty of distractions for long waits and anxious minds.

As I pushed open Wanda's door a woman, seated by the bed glanced back at me. She stood up and walked over to greet me.

"Hi, are you Jennie?" she asked in a hushed tone.

"Yes," I said.

"I'm Caroline. Thank you for coming so quickly."

We walked together toward the bed while I kept my emotions in check. If I became too empathetic I would be of no service.

"This is my mother, Wanda," Caroline said as we gazed down at the frail woman swallowed up in the sheets and blankets on the bed. "She's had her eyes closed since yesterday. I talk to her and wonder if she can hear me. The last time she spoke was last night when she called out my father's name."

Caroline took a seat, and I walked around the bed to sit across from her. As I tuned into my surroundings, I sensed a spirit in the room with us. A man materialized behind Caroline, standing in my symbolic place for father, and I saw a letter *G* on his chest.

"I see a male spirit who is wearing dark brown trousers and a white long sleeved shirt. His hat shades his face. His name begins with a *G*," I said.

"My father's name was Griffin," she said as she looked around the room. "Where is he?"

"He's standing behind you," I said. The spirit took off his hat, and his eyes seemed familiar. Where had I seen him?

"Hello again," he said, and smiled at me.

'Again? Do I know you?' I telepathically asked him.

He nodded, then moved closer to Wanda.

"Your father is now standing by the head of the bed," I said as I searched my memory for him.

"Hi, Daddy," Caroline said. Then to her mother she said, "Dad's here, Mom. He made it!"

Griffin grinned and said, "Tell Caroline I said *Jinx.*"

"Your father is saying Jinx," I said.

She smiled and said, "Jinx was my cat's name. He bonded with my father, which was funny because Dad never liked cats. But when he'd visit us, Jinx would sit with him. Dad even bought a harness so Jinx could take walks with him. When Dad passed away, Jinx stopped eating. He'd just sit on the back of the chair, gazing out the window, as if looking for him. About a week after Dad died, Jinx passed away."

As Caroline spoke, a cat materialized in Griffin's arms. This seemed familiar too. But why?

'Have I dreamt of you?' I silently asked him.

"Yes," he said. The tabby disappeared, and Griffin gave me a message for his wife.

I looked down at her, and said, "Wanda, Griffin is here. He wants me to tell you there is nothing to fear. He is here to help you."

Caroline choked back a sob. "Her time must be near."

"Yes, could be," I said.

Caroline patted her mother's hand and said, "You can let go, Mom. It's okay to be with Daddy." Then she looked at me and asked, "Why does death hurt so much?"

"You mean to those of us still here?"

"Yes," she said.

"We mourn their physical presence. But death is part of life."

"Why is life so hard?"

"That's relative, isn't it? What's difficult to one, may not be for another. But regardless of how we perceive life, I believe we're not alone at the end of our journey. Each person's met by one or more spirits to guide them home."

"How do we get home?"

"Some who have experienced a near death experience say we go through a tunnel of light."

"What happens when we get there?"

"From what I've learned in my readings, at some point after returning home the spirit has a life review. There, he can evaluate whether his time on Earth served his soul, and how he affected others. From this new perspective he might want to get a message to someone on the Earth plane. Most of the messages I receive have three things in common. First, the spirit wants to tell his loved one he is okay and alive. And if he feels remorse about something he desires to make amends."

"And the third thing?" she asked.

"The spirit desires to help us in some way. This usually involves a letting go of something from the past. We can't experience peace if we are dwelling on resentment, fear or regret. The spirits want to assist us."

"Is a reading the only way we can get a message?"

"No, there are various ways they reach out to us. It might be in something we read, or a flash of inspired thought. Or something we see, smell or hear, such as a glimpse of them, or an identifiable sound, or the smell of their cologne. We might feel them near, or visit with them in dreams. I had a delightful lucid dream in which my father said he approved of my career. So many people are waiting for another's permission to do what they want with their life."

"Well, my dad doesn't need to send me a message. He must know that I think of him as a wonderful father," she said.

"But your father does have a message," I said.

"He does? What is it?"

"He says it's time to focus on your life now. Do things with your children, and take time for your marriage. Go out on date nights."

Caroline sighed. "I can't remember the last time Keith and I had fun, or went out for a romantic dinner."

"Yes, and your father says to stop worrying. Your mother's blessed with happy memories. You've been a good daughter, and he is grateful."

"Thank you, Daddy. I love you so much," Caroline said.

Griffin said, "I love you, too, Peanut."

I repeated this to Caroline, and she said, "Peanut? I haven't heard that nickname in a long time. You most certainly have my father here, Jennie." She looked at her mother and said, "All this makes me ponder my own mortality. Who do you think we are?"

"We are spiritual beings having a human experience."

"Okay," she said, looking back across the bed at me, "but what is a spiritual being?"

"The Greek philosopher Heraclitus said, 'Living and dead are the same'. Did he mean we look the same on both sides of the veil? Or was he referring to us as spiritual beings in both this life and the afterlife?

"I have studied and read much about this. And while I'm convinced that our spirit continues after physical death, I don't have a definitive answer. And my perception is apt to change. Some say that spirit resembles a multi-faceted crystal, and each lifetime adds to or polishes the facets. Some say that spirit is light, energy or electricity. Others say we are celestial beings, similar in look and appearance to human, but vibrating at a finer or higher vibration. I tend to favor that idea. And I've heard other theories as well.

"But all I can say for certain is when I describe a spirit during a reading, he or she will appear as recognizable to the sitter, who is the recipient of the message. And that same spirit's looks can change for different sitters. So, how spirits look when we're not communicating remains a mystery. Regardless, I have always found the spirits to be wise, helpful and loving."

"I wonder why we came to this planet," she said.

"I believe we choose to come here. And our spirits live many incarnations, not just on Earth, but in other realms and dimensions as well. I think life's about unfoldment and experience. My one grandmother was a sailing enthusiast. In a message I received from her, she said she had loved riding the waves, and missed the smell of the salt air and feeling the wind on her skin. She had loved the *experience* of sailing on the sea."

"I see, and what is life really?"

"That's anyone's guess. Is it a movie, where we are cast in a role on some cosmic screen? Or is it a holodeck, where we chose the program we wanted to experience? One entertaining example of that notion was an episode called, *Projections* in season two of the Star Trek Voyager television show.

"And then there's parallel lives. Imagine if each decision creates an alternate life. The number of such paths would be incalculable! Again quoting Heraclitus, 'Lifetime is a child at play, moving pieces in a game'. Whatever life is, I'm not sure why we don't remember while we're in it."

"You gave me a lot to think about," Caroline said.

"Yes, and just when I think I've figured it out, something shifts my perspective," I said. "Perhaps not knowing is part of life's mystery and wonder."

Caroline nodded, and was about to respond, when her mother spoke. We both gazed down at Wanda, and Caroline said, "Did she just say angel?"

CHAPTER THREE

A BRIGHT CIRCLE appeared on the wall near the foot of the bed. I looked over at Caroline. She didn't seem to be aware of it. I looked back at the circle which had grown into a large portal.

A tall celestial being stepped from the portal into the room. She was radiant and magnificent and when she gazed down at me I felt bliss.

The being looked at Wanda. She took several breaths, then went still. I watched as Wanda's spirit rose up and out of her physical body, and morphed to reflect her features and form. With a shimmer, her celestial body morphed again, and appeared younger and full of vitality. Griffin greeted her, and together they followed the spiritual guardian into the irradiant portal.

I was so mesmerized by the scene, I was drawn into it too, and astral traveling with them in the celestial tunnel. A dazzling light radiated in the distance and I yearned to go to it. And the closer we neared the light, the stronger that desire grew.

But my forward motion slowed, then stopped as Wanda, Griffin, and the being sped ahead. I looked back to find the source of what was impeding me. There was a cord attached from my spirit, down through the portal and into my body. I tugged at it, but couldn't pull free. I glanced back at the others, willing myself to catch up to them. But they were far ahead of me now. I wanted to go home, too. I didn't want to go back, and gave the cord another tug.

A discarnate voice said, "It's not your time!" And I was back in my body, seated across from Caroline. She was staring at me.

"Are you okay?" she said. "I've been talking to you, and you haven't answered me."

"Yeah, I'm okay," I said with a twinge of homesickness as I glanced at the wall where the portal had been.

Mica was at my ear, "It wasn't your time to go. You have work to do."

'I don't care, I want to go home', I thought back to Mica as I crossed my arms and pouted.

"Think about Jake and your family," Mica said.

A vision of my loved ones came to mind, and snapped me out of my malaise. I wasn't ready to leave them; not yet.

"Did you see Mother's spirit when she passed away? Is that why you got so quiet?" Caroline asked.

I nodded as the door to the room flung open, and a RN rushed in to check on Wanda and the monitors.

"Did she go with Daddy?"

"Yes," I said as the nurse looked at us. "Let's get you out of here."

Caroline was pale and trembling as I helped her to her feet. She was taller and heavier than me and I hoped she wouldn't faint. I ushered her from the room and waved at Keith who ran over to us.

"Is she gone?" he asked.

"Yes, and your wife needs to sit down," I said, relieved as he took her from me.

Caroline cried as he escorted her to the waiting room. They sat on a sofa together, and hugged. "Daddy was here," she said between sobs.

"He was?" Keith asked, looking at me.

"Yes," I said, and took a chair facing them. "Her father and another spirit guided her home."

"I don't understand how you do what you do, Jennie. But thank you for sitting here with me," Caroline said, "it really helped."

"I'm happy to be of service," I said, not sure how I do what I do either. But a spirit voice in that tunnel had made it quite clear that I still had time to figure it out. "If you ever need to talk, give me a call," I said, and handed her a business card.

☼

As I waited for the elevator I reflected on the portal, the shimmering celestial being, and the tunnel. It seemed it was all brilliant light.

"Do you have a business card?"

I turned to see the nurse that had been in Wanda's room.

"Yes, of course," I said. I pulled a card from my purse and handed it to her.

She pocketed it and walked away.

The doors opened, and I stepped into the elevator and rode it down. When the doors opened on the first floor, I didn't know the way to my car. In following Keith to Wanda's room, I had paid no attention.

"Which way?," I asked as I stood in the hallway, facing east. Unsure, I turned to face west and detected a gentle nudge at my back. West it was and walked down the long winding corridor.

When I stepped into the lobby I marveled at the sunlit atrium. How had I not noticed the glass walls, skylights, tall trees and lush plants earlier? I pulled my cell phone from my purse, and the moment I switched it on the ringer it rang. I glanced at the caller ID as I answered, "Hi, Jake."

"I left several messages. You had me worried."

"Sorry, I had silenced my phone."

"Well, it's good to hear your voice. You didn't say in your note why you had to leave early."

"Oh, it's been an amazing morning. I'm heading back to the office to write it all in my journal."

"What? Where are you?"

"I'm at the hospital."

"Why? Are you okay?"

"Yes, I'm fine. A Caroline Werther asked me to come to the hospital. She wanted to know if her father's spirit had come for her mother, as he promised. He was there, and with another spirit, they escorted her mother into a portal, where they traveled toward a brilliant light. I astral traveled in the tunnel with them!"

"You did? Sounds fascinating, and I can't wait to hear more."

"Oh, you will," I said. "And it was so romantic how Griffin, that's Caroline's father, came back for his wife. So I was wondering..."

"About what?"

"If you go first, will you come back for me?"

"You have to ask?"

I smiled into the phone, comforted to know he'd at least try. Jake and I first met last fall when he came in for a reading. We married on New Year's Eve at the Del Vista Clubhouse, surrounded by family and friends. After our honeymoon in North Carolina, I moved out of the apartment at the back of my store and into Jake's home in the Country Club Estates. He helps manage the pro shop there, and is passionate about golf. I'm passionate about Jake, my career, my store, and my family.

CHAPTER FOUR

WHEN I RETURNED to my office I typed everything that had occurred that morning into my journal. Once I had typed every detail, I kicked off my shoes, and laid down on the sofa for a nap.

I dreamt I was standing on a celestial pathway of illuminated light, suspended in space near the moon. As I walked along the strands of light, I came upon a lush garden. I tiptoed around it, admiring the colorful flowers and butterflies.

In the center of the garden was a pond full of goldfish, and a tumbling fountain at its center. As I sat on the bench near it, an illuminated being appeared. He was very tall, and smiled at me as he sat next to me.

"Who are you?"

"I am one of your guides. I'm here to discuss your experience with Wanda," he said.

"What can you tell me about that?"

"It was not unusual for Wanda to be escorted home. The newly departed are met by one or more spirits, whatever their manner of passing."

"That's comforting," I said. "And can you tell me about the cord that held me to my body?"

"The cord you refer to is the Silver Cord. It is the link between the higher self and the body."

"I'm glad I didn't sever it," I said.

"Tas it was not your time."

"And what about that tunnel?"

"Not all who pass perceive a tunnel. But in the tunnel of Wanda's passing was the loving arms of spirits welcoming her home; just as she imagined it would be."

"It felt so good there," I said with a twinge of homesickness. "So was home the bright light I saw in the distance?"

"No, the light you refer to is a gateway."

"Who told me to go back to my body? Was it you?"

"Yes, and you became aware of Caroline talking to you."

"No wonder she looked at me so oddly when I returned to my body," I said and stared at the fountain. "What is it like at death?"

"When the spirit lifts out of the body it can feel like a release, especially if the body was ailing or painful. If the spirit looks at his body, he might not at first recognize himself. He'll look quite different in 3D than he did in his reflection or a photograph. If the departed thinks of a loved one still on the Earth, in that thought he will be in her presence. If the loved one senses his spirit, she'll likely attribute it to imagination. At some point, the departed will become aware that someone from spirit is calling to him.

"His spirit greeter might be someone he knew on the Earth plane, who predeceased him. This greeter will answer any questions the newly departed spirit might have, and then suggest they go home. But the spirit decides when to go home. He may choose to stay and watch his funeral or other event, or see about someone or a circumstance. This is his choice; but he is not stuck or lost," he said.

We gazed at the goldfish in the pond, and he said, "It's kind of like how a swimmer at the bottom of a swimming pool knows the way to the surface. All souls hear the call home, and the spirit greeters are ready to escort them."

"Where is home?"

"The afterlife is a higher frequency than your realm. This vibratory separation is what is referred to as the veil."

That made sense, and since working as a medium I've become more aware of vibration and the subtle energies. But something more Earthly was bothering me, so as long as I was getting guidance, I asked, "Why is Evonne so nasty toward me? What did I ever do to her?"

"It's not about you, it's about her."

"Well, it sure seems to be about me."

"You are a trigger, reminding her that she didn't get her way. She is used to being in control, especially of Ben. When he married you against her wishes, she was enraged that he had crossed her. But rather than blame her darling boy, she targets her anger at you."

"So it is about me!"

"No, it's about her. You are not the cause, just the trigger."

I wasn't sure what to make of that, so asked a new question. "Why do I so rarely hear from my mother?"

"Fear not, she is well and keeps busy," he said. I guess I didn't look too happy with that reply, as he added, "She is okay and you will see her when you come home. Until then, she looks in on you at times. But the person you refer to as your mother was just one aspect of her higher self. Life is not all that mysterious, but is difficult for the mortal mind to grasp. The human brain does not hold the answers you seek. Go within, and meditate more."

"Can you tell me who you are?"

"I am one of your guides, and we assist you from an agreement made before your birth. And at times, you have served as a guide in one of our incarnations. We progress as we help each other. This is not unusual as no person is alone. All are guided."

"Am I living my life purpose?"

"Your purpose is your passion. Follow your joy, bliss and love. The future is not promised, so live each day to the fullest. Don't wait for things to improve or get different or get better to appreciate your life. Be present and happy now. Again I suggest that you meditate more often to tap into your intuitive Truth."

"Anything else?"

"Just make meditation a priority. The more you connect with your higher self, the stronger your intuition, and the more you'll enjoy this journey."

☼

The last thing I remembered as I awoke from the dream was thanking him. With no readings until this afternoon, now seemed a good time as any to meditate.

I sat up with my feet flat on the floor, hands resting in my lap. I closed my eyes and took a deep breath, relaxing into the seat. I released the tension in my neck by touching my ear to my right shoulder, then stretched the left side. Balancing my head at center, I took another deep breath, and settled in.

I focused on my breathing, and relaxed more with each breath. Shifting my awareness to my heart I imagined a bright beam of light... of Divine Love... streaming in from the heavens, into that chakra. My heart center glowed and expanded as I acknowledged receiving and sending out love. I imagined the Love radiating around and within me, like a cocoon of pulsating energy.

The Light filled my office, my store and flowed out to the street. It expanded across town, across my country and dipped in and out of each ocean. It circled the globe, shot off the Earth at lightning speed, then returned and illuminated my third eye. There was no longer a sense of boundary or an edge to me. I felt peaceful and resonated in this blissful state.

Twenty minutes later, I opened my eyes, and a thought popped into my mind. I glanced at my watch. "Oh no!"

I jumped to my feet, grabbed my purse and ran down the hallway. Megan was standing behind the counter as I ran out the door saying, "I'm late meeting Kate for lunch!"

CHAPTER FIVE

KATE AND I had made plans to meet for lunch at The Patio, her favorite restaurant since childhood. We hadn't spoken in nearly a week, so I looked forward to catching up with her.

When I entered the restaurant, the manager greeted me. "Hello, Mrs. Walker, it's good to see you again."

"You too, Marcus. I'm meeting Kate. Is she here?"

"Yes, Miss Kate is on the patio." His phone rang at his podium, and he said, "Let me answer this and I'll take you to her."

"That's okay, I'll find her," I said as he answered his phone. I walked through the dining area, admiring the murals, chairs and tables. Someone had hand painted every surface with palm trees, birds, butterflies and tropical fish. And someone had a green thumb. The place was nearly overgrown with lush plants and flowers that accented the restaurant's theme.

As I stepped out onto the back patio, I saw my daughter seated at one of the umbrella tables, sipping a glass of iced tea. I took a seat across from her as Libby, the waitress, came to the table and handed me a menu. I asked for a lemonade, and Libby went to get my drink while I read the menu.

"I thought you had forgotten about our lunch," Kate said. "I was just about to call you."

"No, I didn't forget."

"So what kept you?"

I was surprised by her agitated tone and set down my menu. "Am I that late?"

Kate sniffed. "Not in your world, I guess."

"What's that supposed to mean?"

"It means that you are notorious for setting out for a place at the exact time you should be arriving."

"I'm sorry if I've upset you. Have you waited long?"

"About fifteen minutes," she said, removing her glasses.

"Have you been crying?"

She nodded as she wiped her tears away with her hands.

"What's wrong?"

"What's wrong? What's always wrong?"

"Is this about Brad?"

She nodded and put her glasses back on as Libby set my drink on the table.

"Are you ladies ready to order?" Libby asked.

"Give us a minute," I said. As Libby walked away, I said, "Are you okay? Want to talk about it?"

"I miss Brad so much," Kate said as she wept.

I searched my purse for tissues and handed her some.

She removed her glasses to dry her eyes, and said, "Will it ever get easier?"

"It's going to take time. It's been less than two months, and you and Brad were very close. It's only natural to miss someone you loved that much."

"I guess you're right," she said, dabbing at her eyes. "And you really need to set an alarm or something to get to places on time."

I didn't respond knowing that most of her anger wasn't directed at me.

Libby returned to our table, and I had to smile as Kate ordered the tropical salad without glancing at the menu she memorized years ago.

"That sounds good, make that two salads," I said, then to Kate I said, "So how are you doing?"

"I have better moments, but overall its been rough."

"I understand. I miss him, too. Not in the same way you do, of course, but I miss having him as my son-in-law."

"He was fond of you too, Mom."

I had debated about sharing something with her, and decided to go for it. "His passing has weighed on my mind. Even as a Spiritualist I've had trouble dealing with it, unable to understand it. But I gained an insight I'd like to share with you."

"What is it?"

"I woke up one morning from an unusually deep sleep. I couldn't recall dreaming, but a word was on my mind."

"What was the word?"

"*Enigma*."

"That's odd."

"Yes, I thought so too. But I've found that when spirit wants me to pay attention, I'll get a word or phrase that I have to look up. This tells me that it's from spirit and not something I invented."

"That makes sense, and you're telling me that gives me goose bumps."

"Yes, well I had chills that morning too, and when I looked up the word it meant, 'puzzling, a mystery, a corundum'. I meditated on the word, seeking how it related to my life. And I realized it referred to Brad. His passing wasn't for me to figure out. I had to let go of asking why, so my grieving could progress."

Kate's eyes filled with tears.

"I didn't tell you this to upset you, Kate. I wanted to share the message that life holds many mysteries; some we'll never figure out. We have to let go, and let the healing in."

She dabbed at her tears, and said, "I guess I'm still harboring guilt. Isn't that what you're referring to?"

"We've discussed this. Why do you still feel guilty?"

"Because he went out for the milk I should've bought earlier that day. If he had stayed home, my children would still have their father."

"If it wasn't the milk, he could've gone to the store for something else."

She looked startled. "What are you saying?"

"Like I said, life holds mysteries. Sometimes we need to let go of guilt, to get on with the grieving process, and on with living."

"But how can I?"

"You must realize this was not your fault. Acknowledge it was out of your control, and that there are things you will not understand. Then let it go. Be patient as you go through the stages of grief. Each day find at least one thing to be grateful for. Keep a journal to facilitate the process."

"What would I write?"

"How about writing that you're grateful for your children?"

"That's a good start."

"Or that you have a nice home."

"Yes, that is a blessing."

"And that you're grateful you knew Brad, and that you were married to him."

"Okay, I see what you mean. Thanks."

Libby returned with our salads. As we ate, Kate said, "You say that our spirit lives on in the afterlife, but how do you know that?"

"I've come to believe this based on what I've experienced, heard and seen in visions, dreams and messages. Others have observed the same things. And plenty of authors and speakers around the globe, from long ago and now, offer the same insights."

"So you haven't wondered if you only see what you want to see?" she said.

"If that were true, how would we explain what happened this morning? Mica woke me from a deep sleep, urging me to get to work earlier than usual. I received a phone call from a woman I never met who asked me to come to her mother's hospital room. While there, I saw her father and her cat in spirit, both of whom appeared in my dreams. I gave her a message about her cat, Jinx, and other things, including a nickname her father called her. I didn't know any of those things beforehand, and didn't expect any of it to happen. So I can't explain it any other way than to say it's coming from the spiritual realms."

"Jinx the cat, huh? Sounds like you had an interesting morning," Kate said.

"Actually, it was amazing to sit with her mother as she made her transition. And that her husband's spirit came for her as he promised. And I watched them follow a luminescent spiritual being through a portal in the wall and up a tunnel."

"Was the being an angel?"

"It's possible. The mother had said angel moments before the being stepped into the room."

CHAPTER SIX

WE FINISHED OUR salads and sat sipping our drinks. Kate said, "I guess Lola has your Gifts. She tells me she's been talking to her dad and that she hears and sees him."

"Well, I communicated with spirits when I was her age, or younger."

"That may be true, but Evan's sad he can't do it."

"At bedtime you might suggest he can visit his father in his dreams and he will remember it when he wakes up. Then, each morning ask him about his dreams, and record them in a journal for him."

"Sounds like a good idea. I'll be happy to do that for him."

"And what about you?"

"What about me?"

"Have you seen or heard Brad?"

"I've had several dreams where I'm with him, I guess. Maybe I should keep a dream journal, too. And I swear, at times I can sense Brad near me. If I turned around, I might see him."

"Then, turn around!"

"I can't."

"Why not?"

"I'm afraid."

"Of what?"

"Of seeing a ghost!"

"Don't be afraid of him. He's just telling you he's okay. And he loves you, he's not trying to scare you."

"Yeah, but still," she said, and bit her lip.

"So what else is new?"

"Oh, I got that teaching job at Evan and Lola's school," she said.

"Congratulations!"

"Thanks, I'm very excited about it! And the best part is, between my new salary and employee discount, I can afford to keep them enrolled there. Without Brad's income I couldn't afford it. But now I can keep them with their school friends and not put them through more changes. So I'm grateful for that."

"That is wonderful news, and another entry for your journal."

She laughed. "Yeah, okay. Now if Lola would just get dressed each morning without argument. With my new job, I'll no longer have the time for her drama."

"Oh? What's up?"

"Every day, she wants to wear her princess costume, complete with the tiara. Her teacher thinks it's just a phase, but this morning I put my foot down. I told her she could only wear it at home, not at school."

"Did she agree?"

"She did, but we'll see. That girl certainly has strong opinions."

"Sounds like someone else I know."

"Who?"

"You! Just wait till she's a teenager, that's when the real fun begins."

"Gee, thanks. It's hard enough raising them on my own when they're this age."

"You're doing great. Stop being so hard on yourself. Now, tell me what my grandson's up to?"

"Evan is focused on Easter. He's been asking me to help write letters to the Easter Bunny, requesting lots of eggs."

"Why does he want eggs?"

"For the Easter Egg hunt."

"Oh, of course. Anything else new with him?"

"Yes, he's been collecting seeds. Whenever we go outside he picks up seeds and puts them in a coffee can. I can't imagine why he's gathering them."

"Who knows? From a past life as a farmer? Or he likes the color or texture of the seeds? Have you asked him?"

"No, I haven't."

"Nathan collected shells, stones and sea glass, as I did as a child. I wouldn't be concerned, and it sounds like Lola and Evan are doing good."

"Yes, other than missing their father, I guess they are doing what kids do."

"Be grateful and happy about your life, Kate. Everyday look for things to be thankful for. And love yourself."

"Love myself? Isn't that narcissistic?"

"Not in the way I mean it. Do you know how during a flight, the attendant will say, in case of emergency put your oxygen mask on first, then help your child?"

"Yes," she said.

"Well, love's kind of like that mask. When we love ourselves, we can give love to others. When we love ourselves, we can stop criticizing ourselves and others. When we love ourselves, we can raise our vibration, attracting more things to be joyful about."

"I'll have to remember that."

"Why not start by being nicer to the person you see in the mirror? You might enjoy reading the book, *You Can Heal Your Life* by Louise Hay."

"Okay, I'll look into it. And I wanted to ask you about meditating. I can't seem to quiet my mind."

"Well, to start sit comfortably so you can relax without your body begging for attention. And place your awareness on your breath as you breathe in and out. You can close your eyes, or keep them loosely focused on something, like a spot on the floor. Experiment to find what works best for you. Try a mantra, repeating a word like God or love or peace," I said. I should have discussed this with her years ago. But it was only recently that she became open to talking about such things. "And you might enjoy the book, *Meditation* by Jane Elizabeth Hart."

"Okay," she said, typing notes for herself using her cell phone.

"There's also active meditation, such as yoga or gardening. By the way, did you ever make an appointment for a reading with Sara Kelsey?" I asked, referring to my mediumship instructor.

"No, not yet," she said. "I'm still thinking about it."

"You could take one of her classes."

"Why? I don't want to be a medium."

"You don't need to become a medium to take her classes. There are plenty of people who attend with no such desire."

"Then what's the point?"

"To experience a connection with spirits, to deepen your intuition, and to learn how to get your own guidance and answers."

"Maybe someday," she said, and sipped her tea. "Oh, I almost forgot to tell you. During dinner the other night, Lola mentioned the name Oliver. I asked who Oliver was, and she said it was Uncle Nathan's new baby.

"So out of curiosity I phoned Nathan. I asked him how Bridgette was feeling. And I asked if they'd chosen a name for the baby. He said they had been weighing names, but had decided on Oliver. I couldn't believe my ears! Should I have told him what Lola said?"

Nathan had never pursued spirituality to my knowledge. But unlike his sister, he had always been open minded and supportive of my Gifts. "I don't see any reason not to tell him. Your brother will likely find it amusing. Let's call him," I said, and dialed his number.

Nathan answered on the second ring. "Hi, Mom."

"Are you free to talk?"

"I have a few minutes."

"Your sister and I are having lunch, and you're on speaker."

"Hi, Nathan," Kate said as she leaned toward the phone.

"Hi, Kate," he said, "what's up?"

"We wanted to tell you that Lola told Kate that your baby's name is Oliver."

"Yeah, so? I told Kate his name the other day," he said.

"Yes, but Lola told me his name before you did," Kate said.

Nathan was silent a moment, then said, "That's quite amazing, and I'll take it as confirmation that our baby likes his name."

CHAPTER SEVEN

AS I EXITED the restaurant, I was looking in my purse for my car keys when a woman approached me and said, "Jennifer, is that you?"

I looked up to see my ex-husband's aunt. "Oh, hello, Cecilia," I said.

"I was on my way to post this letter when I saw you. But I wasn't sure it was you at first, guess we're all getting on in years."

What did she mean by that?

"What brings you downtown?" she said.

"I had lunch with Kate."

"Oh? Is she still here?" she asked, looking around us.

"No, she left ahead of me."

"Sorry I missed her. So you ate at The Patio?"

"Yes," I said. Why else would I have come out of their door?

"The Patio always was her favorite restaurant."

"Yes, I know," I said. Was Cecilia implying she knew my daughter better than me?

"Well, I can't remember the last time I saw you. Haven't seen you around much since you divorced Ben."

Ben had broken up our marriage, not me. But I didn't want to expend energy correcting her, so instead I said, "Yes, it has been awhile."

"I spoke to Ben recently. He's doing really well with his art, you know."

I had heard, but didn't care. "That's good," I said.

"Yes, he's done phenomenally well since he met Jasmine."

Was she trying to rile me? Cecilia, and her pal, my ex-mother-in-law, seemed to enjoy throwing Jasmine in my face. Ben had met her after our divorce. They married several years ago, and she had taken over managing his career from the start. As much as I hated to admit it, she had done what I never could. She helped develop his talents, while keeping his swollen ego in check. And from what I've heard, he's never cheated on her. But he often cheated on me.

"Ben also said the strangest thing," she said. "He told me that you had opened a crystal shop, and you were fortune telling. It's not true, is it?"

"No, I'm a fortuneteller," I said.

"Oh, good, I thought he must be kidding and..."

"I'm a medium," I said, cutting her off.

"What? You're joking!"

"No, I'm not."

"Honestly, what would possess you to do such a thing? And in public?"

"There is nothing wrong with mediumship, Cecilia. I have nothing to hide. I provide a good service, and my clients are referring me."

"Well, I don't see...," she said, obviously flustered. "Well, hopefully you won't be placing our family's good name on your signage now that you've remarried."

I took a deep breath to keep my cool. Ben's family always had their noses in the air, as if they were better than everyone. "When I opened the shop, it was as Jennie Malone."

"What? You don't say!"

"But I've changed the signs to Jennie Walker," I said, swallowing my anger.

"Oh, that is a relief," she said, fanning herself with the envelope she held in her hand. "Now tell me, Jennifer, is this a phase? Is it menopause? Or perhaps its guilt over leaving Ben? Just what is making you act so irrationally?"

"First of all, I have no guilt because I didn't leave Ben. He left me. And, I'm not going through a phase, menopause or revenge on your good family name. Mediumship is my passion, and now my career."

"Career? Oh, you can't be serious!" she laughed, then said, "So tell me, are there ghosts us now?" She twirled for emphasis as she looked around.

"I'm not here for your entertainment, Cecilia. And I don't perform on cue. I choose when, where, and to whom I give messages."

Her hand went to her chest, acting affronted. "Well, you don't have to be so rude!"

"I'm the one being insulted," I said. I had nearly forgotten how expertly she and my ex-mother-in-law could push my buttons. But being as I'm no longer a Malone, there was no reason to stand here or swallow my words. It was time to cut this reunion with this rude woman short.

I was free to walk away, and about to do so when she said, "You've always been too sensitive. I would have thought you would've outgrown that by now."

I was stunned! Why do some people assume they can say anything to you, then feign surprise when you're insulted. I may be sensitive, but she was being insensitive! I took a breath, then said, "See you around, I have to go."

"Oh, stop being so childish. Now, let me ask you, have you heard about Evonne?"

"What about her?"

"She's been sick, and I've been worried about her."

"No one told me."

"Really? I'm surprised Kate didn't tell you."

"How sick is she? Is she in the hospital?"

"You're the psychic, you tell me. Don't you get paid to pick up on things like that?"

I bristled. "I gotta go, like now."

"You could at least be civil. I'm simply trying to have a conversation with you."

"Oh, is that what you call it? Well, I hope Evonne's better soon," I said and turned to leave.

"Wait," she said and grabbed my arm. "Will Evonne be okay? Will she pull through?"

What was going on here? She insults me, then she questions me. Was she sincere in asking me that? "I don't have a clue," I said.

"How can you not know? You're either a psychic or you're not. There's no middle ground, Jennifer, is there?"

Cecilia is one of those individuals who likes to play mind games. She knocks you off balance with a good verbal left hook when you least expect it, and enjoys seeing how you respond. But this conversation was exhausting amidst her vocal thrusts, jabs and retreats.

"Contrary to what you may think, Cecilia, I'm not tuned in all the time."

"Really? Can't you ask your fairies, or whoever or whatever it is you do, to tell you about Evonne?"

Jeez, the woman was mocking me while asking me for help. "Sorry, but my fairies are busy right now. You take care," I said, stepping off the curb while pressing the key fob to unlock my Subaru.

As I slid onto the seat and closed the door I felt insulated, like a barrier had formed between us. Cecilia stood watching me a minute, then walked away.

As I drove toward the Sunflowers Shoppe, I took long slow breaths to calm myself. My cell phone rang, and I answered it without looking at the caller ID. I was instantly sorry I had.

"Jennie!"

"Hello, Ben," I said.

"I received a call from my Aunt Cecilia. She said you were very rude to her."

"Is that what she told you?"

"Yes, and I don't appreciate it. You've no reason to be rude. What's she ever done to you? Why would you go out of your way to upset an old woman?"

"Did it ever occur to you that there are two sides to this?"

"I don't want to hear it."

"You never did."

"I never did what?"

"You've never wanted to listen to my side."

"For being the holy deacon of spirits and all, you should learn to be more civil."

"What did you call me? The holy what of whom?"

"Never mind that."

"Is that what you tell people about me? Talk about rude! Listen, Ben, I'm tired of defending myself to you. And as for your aunt, I tried my best to be civil, but she started it. She delights in agitating everyone, and you know it!"

"Grow up!"

"No, you grow up!"

He disconnected before I could yell at him again, and I tossed the phone to the passenger seat. Damn, I hated the idea of having Karma with that man, and his aunt and his mother, and I may have just added to it!

But wasn't that just like Ben, always walking away in the middle of an accusation. I was reeling, and needed to calm down. I had appointments, and I didn't want to be resonating at this low frequency when I read for my clients.

But I was tired of always having to be on the defensive. Fed up with swallowing my words and anger. I replayed Cecilia's conversation in my head. She had not only started it, she'd been rude and condescending from the start. My cell phone rang again, and I answered it, ready to battle again with Ben.

"Now what!" I said.

"Jennie? What's wrong?"

"Sorry, Jake, I didn't realize it was you."

"And who were you expecting?"

"Ben."

"What did he do now?"

"Oh, he's just being Ben."

"What happened?"

"I ran into his wicked Aunt Cecilia, the sister-in-law of my evil ex-mother-in-law."

"I think I saw that once in a low budget horror film."

I laughed. "Yeah, but instead of playing vampires, they are real energy vampires."

"And what are energy vampires?"

"Energy vampires rile you up so that once you get agitated, they steal your energy. That's why being with them leaves you exhausted."

"So his aunt stole your energy?"

"Something like that."

"You want to talk about it?"

"Not much to tell. I ran into her after lunch. Cecilia was rude, and I had to swallow a lot of anger and words."

"Swallowing angry words is not healthy."

"Yes, I realize that."

"Where does Ben come in?"

"Ben called, accusing me of being rude to his aunt."

"He must have got an earful from her, and took it out on you."

"You're siding with him?"

"No, I'm not taking his side. So tell me, how was your lunch with Kate?"

"It was wonderful and I wish we'd meet more often."

"You need to calendar it in, otherwise time slips away, and its weeks or months later."

"You are right," I said, then in a softer voice added, "Hey, I'm glad you called."

"Yeah?"

"Yeah," I said, smiling into the phone.

"Why's that?"

"Because you've made me calmer. You have a Gift for helping me feel grounded and balanced."

"Well, I don't know how, but I hope I can always do that for you."

"I doubt that'll be a problem because it's not what you do; it's who you are deep inside. And I'm grateful for it. I love you so much."

"I love you too, and I'm glad to be of service."

Invigorated from Jake's call, I drove the last mile to my store feeling gratitude that I was married to him and not Ben. And I was grateful Jake had no relatives like Cecilia… at least none that I've met.

CHAPTER EIGHT

MY JOURNAL WAS expanding as I typed about my latest sessions. One recent client feared the shadows she sees in her bedroom at night.

"It's your spirit friends saying hello," I said.

"Well, they are scaring the heck out of me," she said, "and I can't sleep."

"Just tell them, 'Thanks for stopping by, but I need my sleep, so go away."

She looked surprised. "It's okay to talk to them like that?"

"Of course, and don't worry, they won't be offended. And they will back off."

Another client was troubled by her cat's ghost. "I sense him around the house. The other night, I nearly tripped over him, before reminding myself he wasn't really there. Why is this happening?" she asked.

"Just acknowledge him," I said. "He's letting you know he's okay."

Such readings were fascinating, but it's sad that people fear spirits trying to say hello.

Someone stepped into my office, and I swiveled my chair to see who it was. Half expecting to see a ghost, it was only Megan. "What's up?" I asked.

"Deanna's on the phone."

"Thank you, I'll take it," I said. I had been meaning to call my friend. We hadn't spoken since my wedding. Deanna and I had met years ago, during mediumship training. Last fall she sublet the office across the hall from mine. But it didn't take her long to decide she didn't like to give readings. Instead, she found her passion by helping private investigators and the police solve cold cases. She preferred working alone, and behind the scenes, but I hoped she'd someday return to work here.

I picked up the phone, and said, "Hello, Deanna. How are you?"

"I'm good. How about you? How was the honeymoon?"

"Heavenly," I said. "I loved being in the mountains of North Carolina, and the Inn was so quaint. Jake and I hiked to several waterfalls, and enjoyed delicious meals at various eateries. We also took a tour of the Biltmore Estate which was beautifully decorated for the holidays."

"Sounds romantic. And how's married life?"

"Being with Jake has been wonderful."

"No surprises then? He's not a nag or worse?"

"No, he's not revealed any nasty traits or habits, and he even claims he doesn't mind that I've cluttered his house. I guess, about the only thing he keeps bringing up is that he'd like for me to play golf with him."

"I didn't know you played golf."

"I haven't played in years, but for his sake, I might give it a try… someday."

"Ah, the blissful newlyweds. And what about your work, any interesting readings lately?"

I recapped the highlights of recent sessions, then told her about my astral traveling in the tunnel with Wanda.

"Amazing!" she said.

"What about you, any interesting cases?"

"Well, as you know, I usually work cold cases. But last week a woman phoned me to help find her husband. Their dog had come home from its walk without him. She told me she suspected the dog was trying to tell her something. It kept staring at her as it paced near the door."

"What did you tell her?"

"I told her she didn't need a psychic to tell her to put a leash on that dog and he'd lead her to her husband. It seemed obvious the dog was trying to tell her that very thing."

"I guess she didn't realize it in her stressful state."

"No, she didn't, and she asked me where he was. An image flashed into my mind of a man laying on the ground next to a gnarled old tree. He was in pain, and couldn't stand up. I told her what I saw. She said it sounded like an abandoned grove near their house.

"About two hours later, she phoned me from the hospital. Their dog had led her to the grove, and that is where she found her husband. He told her he couldn't call for help because the battery on his cell phone was dead, so he didn't take it on his walk. He confirmed he had sent their dog, Jet, home for help. Isn't that something?"

"Yes, but why was he in the hospital?"

"He had tripped over a tree root in the dark, landed on a rock, and fractured his hip."

"Ouch! That must have been painful."

"Yes, I guess so. And that's why he couldn't stand up."

"And what about Jet?"

"What do you mean? He wasn't hurt."

"No, but the dog should've been richly rewarded for getting help."

"Oh, I agree and I asked her. She said Jet was getting a large steak for dinner."

"It must have felt gratifying to help that man get found."

"Yeah, it was a happy ending, unlike most cold cases I work on."

"Hey, helping a family get closure is being of service, too," I said.

"I guess that's true."

"Well, if you ever want to come back here, your office is waiting."

"Thanks, and I appreciate your offer, but I prefer what I'm doing."

"Understood," I said. "Well, we've been chatting away, was there a reason you called?"

"Yes, I almost forgot. Sara is hosting a workshop, and I hoped you'd go with me."

"Oh? What is it about?"

"Spoon bending."

"Spoon bending? Why would Sara teach that?"

"According to her flier, it's about energy and faith and belief."

"Sounds interesting. Have you ever bent a spoon?"

"No, and I'm itching to try. You know Sara's classes are great fun, and she's even providing the spoons."

"When is it?"

"Tomorrow night."

"That's short notice, but, why not. I'm game if you are."

"Great, you can ride with me. I'll pick you up at your store."

"Okay, see you then."

☼

I looked forward to seeing Sara and Deanna again. But spoon bending? Isn't that something a magician would study? And what does it have to do with mediumship?

Well, whatever; Sara's class was sure to be informative and fun.

CHAPTER NINE

MEGAN CAME TO my office and said, “Got a minute?”

“Of course, what’s up?”

"It’s about Chad,” she said. “He’s asked me to move in with him, but I wanted to at least be engaged before we lived together. So I asked him how committed he was and he got angry. Why would that make him mad? Doesn’t he plan to marry me? What do you think?”

Megan stared at me, waiting for an answer, so I decided to toss the question back at her. “What are your thoughts?”

“That he’s a coward who won’t admit that he doesn't want to marry me. He says living together is a commitment, but I want more. What would you do?”

Jeez, I really didn’t want to get involved. Megan had met Chad a few months ago when he came in for a reading. There had been an instant attraction, and they had dated ever since. “Why not hold off moving into his place? What’s the rush?”

“If he doesn't want to marry me, he must not love me. Why bother even dating?”

“Isn’t it possible that you could be overreacting? Perhaps you are reading too much into it. Maybe to Chad, moving in together is a big commitment, even if it’s not the one you wanted.”

"You're siding with him?"

I held up my hand. "I'm not taking sides. I'm suggesting that you reevaluate the situation. You've been so happy together. You don't want to lose something so special over a matter of miscommunication."

"Is that it?"

"It's possible," I said, wishing for a diversion when the wind chimes peeled out over the front door. "Is someone here?"

Megan stepped out to the hallway and looked toward the storefront. "Yes, guess your next appointment's here," she said.

Megan walked down the hall and returned within minutes with a young woman she introduced as Taylor.

"Welcome," I said, "please take a seat."

Taylor settled into the chair and looked at me with large luminescent eyes. Her smile showed perfect white teeth, and her long hair cascaded around her sweet oval face. I've always wished for such thick, long locks.

I noticed her polished nails, then glanced at mine. I hadn't had a manicure since my wedding. But I reined in my thoughts, and said, "How can I help you, Taylor?"

"I'm here to visit my grandmother. Is she here?"

A spirit materialized behind Taylor's chair and stepped into my symbolic location for grandmother. She appeared youthful and fit, unlike the stereotypical matron I'm used to seeing. "Yes, she is here. She looks young," I said.

"Everyone always thought she was much younger than she was. Grandma always said it was her genes and the greens," she said with a soft southern drawl.

"The greens?"

"Yeah, Grandma drank a lot of green smoothies, you know, blending kale, spinach and other greens with fruit. She left me her blender and now I'm drinking them, too."

I looked at her youthful looking grandmother and made a renewed commitment to add more green smoothies to my diet.

The spirit nodded at me, indicating she was ready to start the session. She showed me a vision of a barn followed by a nearly blinding flash of light. I told Taylor what I saw, and added, "I sense this has to do with her passing."

"Yes, there was a violent storm and while Grandpa put the horses in the barn, Grandma was fighting with Molasses to go in there, too."

"Molasses?"

"Yeah, it's what Grandma called the horse. Grandpa named him something else, a name I don't even remember now, when it was born. But Grandma always said that horse was as stubborn and slow as molasses, and the name stuck. Anyway, she was out in the pasture tugging at him and calling to him to follow her to the barn when lightning struck them."

So that bright flash of light was a new symbol for me, and I mentally filed it away as her grandmother sent me a block of thought. "Your grandmother wants you to find comfort in that she didn't suffer. Her spirit was out of the body before the lightning hit. This is typical, during a fatal tragedy the spirit does not suffer."

"That's good to know," she said.

Her grandmother placed a virtual object in my hand. I studied it, and said, "Your grandmother is showing me a rag doll. It looks handmade with yellow straw hair sticking out from under its blue hat. It has a soft puffy face with large button eyes, soft floppy arms and legs. It is wearing a pink shirt and blue jeans."

"You just described Annabelle! My grandmother made her for me," she said. "I'm sorry I put her in storage, Grandma. It's not that I didn't like the doll."

"No need to be sorry, Taylor," I said. "Your grandmother is showing the doll as evidence she is here with you."

"Evidence? What does that mean?"

"It means she is providing symbols and clues to me so I can give you information to show she is really here."

"Oh, well, I never doubted that. I mean isn't that what you do, you know, talk to spirits?"

I smiled. "Yes, but I offer evidential mediumship and don't just tell you what you want to hear."

"Oh, okay, I get it. Well, is she happy?"

"Yes, she says she is happy, and she looks it."

"That's good, and I have a question for her."

"Okay, what is it?"

"Ask Grandma if I should marry Garrett or James."

I sat back, surprised that another person would ask me about her love life so soon after Megan had questioned me about hers. "You came here to ask who you should marry?"

"Yes," she said.

"I'm sorry, but I'm not a fortuneteller."

"That's fine, but I'm not asking you, I'm asking Grandma."

"Look, I don't dabble in predictions."

"Why not?"

"Well, for one thing, you are in charge of your life. You shouldn't ask anyone, not even Grandma, who to marry. For another thing, life is a process and if I gave you your answers, I'd rob you of your own unfoldment. Lastly, there are the timelines."

"The what lines?"

"The timeline theory is that we have unlimited future paths, or timelines, based on our decisions. Each decision can lead to another path. For example, say that a psychic tells you that you are going to meet a guy named Mike. The next day as you are driving to work, you debate about stopping at a convenience store for a snack. You decide to not stop, as you don't want to be late for work. If you had stopped at the store, you would have met Mike, as the psychic had predicted. Instead you chose, by your free will, to drive straight to work going along a different timeline or outcome."

"So I won't meet Mike?"

"No, but if he was an integral part of your life journey, you'd meet another day or at different location. This would be an alternate path from the one at the convenience store; creating a different story of how you met. You see? There are numerous possibilities."

"Okay," she said, "so you're saying to stop at the store tomorrow morning to meet Mike? Is that who I should marry?"

She certainly had selective hearing. "I'm not saying that I foresee you with anyone named Mike. I was just giving you an example."

"Oh now I'm really confused. Are you saying I won't marry Garrett or James? That there's someone else?"

I shook my head. "Look, marriage is a major decision and requires your serious consideration."

Taylor sighed. "Grandma and Grandpa had such a great marriage. They were married over forty years. They made it look so easy. I want a husband like that."

Her grandmother's spirit pointed toward her heart. I nodded as I received her message and said, "How do you feel when you are with James?"

Taylor looked up at me with a furrowed brow and shrugged. "I am happy with him. James is always a gentleman and takes me to fancy restaurants and buys me beautiful flowers. I really like that."

"How do you feel about Garrett?"

Taylor smiled and said, "Garrett makes me laugh, and he likes to do unusual things. Two weeks ago he took me to meet up with a couple of his friends and we went mudding in his truck. It was so messy, but so much fun! Last weekend, he stopped on our way to the beach to buy take-out. He spread a blanket on the sand and we sat watching the waves while we ate dinner.

"As the sun set, he told me about the space station. He said that he signed up to get email alerts from NASA and the space station was flying over our area that night. He brought out binoculars, and we laid on the blanket looking up at the stars. And then we saw it fly by really fast."

"So tell me, what if you never saw Garrett again?"

"Why? Is something bad going to happen to him?"

"No, I'm not saying that. I'm saying, for whatever reason, you decide to never see him again, how would you feel?"

"I'd be sad. Garrett is so much fun, and is always surprising me with new adventures."

"What if you never saw James again?"

"I'd miss him, but in a different way. James would never go mudding. The only time he goes to the beach is to swim. He's so serious, but a great guy, a straight walker."

"A straight walker?" I asked, never before hearing that phrase.

"Yes, what Grandma would call a just man."

"So if you could foresee the future, say five years from now, which path would you prefer; one with James or Garrett or someone else?"

She chewed her lip as she contemplated this a few minutes, then smiled and said, "I'd like to have more dinners on the beach."

"You just got your own guidance."

"I did? Thank you, Jennie!"

Thank you, Grandma.

After Taylor left, I searched online for NASA alerts about the International Space Station. The ISS would be passing over our area that evening. I phoned Jake and said, "I'd like to sit with you on a blanket in our backyard tonight. I have a surprise to show you after it gets dark."

"Man, I love when you talk dirty," he said.

Later that night, Jake and I sat in the backyard gazing up at the heavens with binoculars. Something brighter than the stars and higher than an airplane appeared in the southern sky, and passed quickly into the Northeast. It was thrilling to see the ISS.

Being such a pleasant night, we decided to linger outside. It was the first time I had been in our backyard and found it so secluded that I offered Jake another, more intimate, surprise.

CHAPTER TEN

FLORIDA'S COOL DRY winters offer the deep level sleeping that I crave. And I was enjoying such a sleep when Jake's alarm buzzed.

He reached over and hit the snooze button, then in unison we turned onto our side and I hugged him. I found cuddling to be one of the perks of being newlywed. He turned off the alarm a second time, and rolled onto his back. I snuggled up under his arm, resting my head on his chest.

"I don't want to get up. You feel too good," Jake said, and hugged me closer.

"You do, too," I said. "I can sneak in a few more minutes if you can."

It didn't take much persuading for him to reset the alarm, and his rhythmic breathing told me he had fallen back to sleep. But I was wide awake, and looked at the furnishings in the room.

Before our marriage, I lived in the apartment at the back of my store. Megan had my things moved here for me while we were on our honeymoon. The only other thing I brought was my Subaru. And while I liked this house, it wasn't mine.

"What are you thinking?" he said.

I hadn't realized he had been watching me. "About my move into your home," I said.

"You mean our home. This is your home too, right?"

I shrugged.

"What can we do to make it more your home?"

I glanced around the room, and said, "Can I change the curtains?"

"You don't like the curtains?"

"Can I hang new wallpaper?"

"What's wrong with the wallpaper?" He laughed. "If changing all that makes you happy, go for it."

"And I can get new living room lamps?"

"Anything else?"

"I'd like to replace the light above the dining room table, and hang a few paintings and a wall hanging."

"How much is this going to cost me?"

"Not much, and if you don't mind, I'd like to hang a photo arrangement of my grandchildren on the living room wall."

"I don't mind, is that it?"

"For now," I said, and kissed him.

"Okay, then let me share what's been on my mind this morning."

"Oh? What's that?" I asked as he placed my hand on his groin. "Do we have time for that?"

"Not if you keep asking questions," he said. "Now, how about slipping out of that nightie."

I happily complied. With Jake sex was stimulating and exciting. And I wasn't self-conscious. He made me feel beautiful as he caressed and looked at me.

I quivered in response to his touch. His love making reminded me of a song by the group Heart. Jake had magic hands, and I released so powerfully it was as if I astral traveled through the roof and above the Earth. The euphoric sensations lingered as he entered me, and we fell into a rhythm. As I gazed up at his handsome face and admired his broad chest, he released.

He rolled off, panting, and said, "Now that's what I call a good morning."

I had to agree.

We cuddled a few minutes longer, when I looked over at the clock. "I gotta go," I said and jumped from the bed.

While I showered Jake shaved. While he showered, I dried my hair and dabbed makeup on my face.

☼

During breakfast Jake looked deep in thought.

"What are you thinking?" I said.

He frowned. "I've been trying to remember the name of the group that sang the song that's been stuck in my head since yesterday."

I laughed. "It'll be harder to get the name if you keep grasping at it. Let it come to you. Just like in getting messages or intuition, it comes in when you let go."

Jake smiled. "Well, regardless of the group's name, what I really want is to get the song out of my head."

"Is it a good song?"

"It's an okay tune, but there's not any song that I want to hear repeatedly."

"Maybe the song has a message. Pay attention to the lyrics."

"Let me sing it to you."

"No, don't do that."

"Why not?"

"Because I don't want the song stuck in my head."

He laughed, and said, "Okay, but there's something I want to ask you."

"What is it?"

"Will you play golf with me Sunday morning?"

"Oh, I haven't played in years."

"How about riding around in the cart with me?"

"Is that allowed?"

"Sure, why not? And you could bring your camera."

"That sounds like fun," I said. I hadn't used my SLR in months. I had always liked photography, but lately I've only taken pictures with my cell phone's camera. This would be a good opportunity to use my Digital Rebel.

☼

The traffic during my drive to work was more congested than usual. One great perk of living at the apartment had been no commute, but living with Jake was worth the trip.

As I entered the store, Megan asked me to go over inventory with her. When we were done, I went to my office and shut the door. I sat in my chair, closed my eyes, and drifted into meditation.

When the inner door appeared I stepped through it, and into my familiar garden. There were trees, flowers, birds and butterflies. I looked up at the blue sky and the white fluffy clouds, then at the waterfront gazebo. I walked up its steps and took a seat, waiting to see who would join me.

A spirit materialized next to me on the bench, and I was delighted to see it was my mother. She made her transition several years ago, and I missed her.

When she first passed away, sensing her near confused me. This was before my training, and she had raised me to not use my Gifts, so it was a frightening experience.

At the time, a friend gave me his appointment with a medium. The medium told me that someday I'd miss that feeling of closeness. I didn't understand what he meant then, but I do now.

We are more than a physical body. We have an astral body, an emotional body and a mental body. The etheric field is what feels familiar to us, just like when we know who is standing behind us, without having to turn around. When my mother first passed away, she was trying to tell me she was okay, and still very much alive.

I communicated with her infrequently now. Her etheric field had raised in vibration, no longer palpable like when she first passed. So to visit with her at my gazebo was a real treat!

"Hello, Mom," I said, "I haven't seen you in a while. Have you been busy?"

She smiled and nodded as she looked at me. "Yes, but I help you and the family as much as I can. I'm aware that you have another grandchild coming."

"Yes, Nathan's son will soon be born."

"And I'm happy you're using your Gifts and being of service. When you were a child I didn't understand it, but didn't mean to block you."

"Well, I've learned that we pick our birth parents, so I might have chosen you for that challenge."

"Yes," she said, "and it's wonderful you've overcome that obstacle."

"I hold you no ill will, Mom. You did the best you knew how, and you acted without malice. I miss you."

She smiled at me, and said, "I'm as close as Lola's smile, Evan's laugh and Emily's hug."

That was comforting. "And the butterflies?" I said.

She laughed. "Oh, yes, and all the yellow butterflies I send your way."

CHAPTER ELEVEN

REBECCA STEVENS LOOKED familiar, and when she took her seat I realized why. She was the nurse that had been in Wanda's room, and at the elevator. She looked different dressed in blue jeans and a T-shirt, and her hair no longer pulled back.

"We met at the hospital," she said.

"Yes, I remember. How can I help you?"

"I've been sensing things around the hospital. I'm afraid the place is full of ghosts."

"You are a sensitive."

She frowned.

"It means you are sensitive to energies and emotions. You know, like being able to sense a person's mood. You are just picking up on the energy."

"So there are ghosts at the hospital?"

"Could be vibrational remnants of event memories."

"What does that mean?"

"An energy remnant is just an apparition, a playback of something that happened. Kind of like a movie that keeps replaying. Let me give you an example.

"Years ago, our family toured a historical aircraft carrier. When we entered the ship's hospital I felt an emotional charge, and had a vision of corpsmen attending to the wounded. I lost sense of time, space and dimension, and became disoriented. At the time, I didn't understand what was happening, and asked to be escorted outside.

"Likewise, you could be sensing energetic remnants at the hospital. Or it could be spirit helpers waiting to take someone home. Or spirits looking in on or assisting loved ones. Or the spirits of patients who have just made their transition. So there's a lot of energy there."

"But, I don't want to see or feel ghosts. I'm afraid of them!"

"They mean you no harm. But if you are uncomfortable, ask the spirits to back off."

"I can do that?"

"Yes, you are in charge of your space. And speaking of spirits, there is a man in spirit waiting to say hello to you. He shows himself as bald with bushy sideburns, a rather bulbous nose, and thick reading glasses. He says that he liked to read the newspaper."

"Oh, I remember him! He was one of my patients," she said with a smile. "He read the obituary every day. He told me that after he turned sixty he became obsessed about his own mortality."

I nodded. "Yes, he says he wasted years of his life worrying about his death. He says it's better to live and enjoy each day than to live worrying about dying. He thanks you for the care you gave him, especially during his final hours."

"I stayed with him that night after my shift ended. His family lived out of state and I didn't want him to die alone."

"He was aware you were there, and he wanted to thank you."

"I was happy to do that for him. Can I ask a question?"

"Certainly," I said.

"Is it okay to ask someone in spirit for help? Like my grandfather? I don't want to pester him."

"When calling on someone in spirit, call on him like you would leave a message on his phone. Tell him what's going on, and then say something like, 'Granddad if you can help me with this, I'd appreciate it.' Then let the matter go.

"There are many spiritual levels and realms, and those in spirit can be busy. So, place your call realizing his answer may not come right away. And it might come in a dream or something you read or hear. Just trust that, if your grandfather can help, he will. Or he will send someone who can."

"That reminds me of what happened yesterday. I was wondering about something, and I received not one, but three email messages on the subject. It certainly got my attention, and now I wonder if it was Grandpa's doing."

"We often think we're not getting our answer, even when it's right in front of us," I said. "It reminds me of a scene in the movie, *The Man With Two Brains* starring Steve Martin. His character asks his departed wife to give him a sign if he should marry a certain woman. His wife's spirit yells no while the lights flicker and her portrait spins. But it's not the answer he wants."

Rebecca laughed, then asked, "How do you communicate spirits?"

"During a reading, my connection is kind of like fine tuning a radio dial. The spirit communicator will look and act in a way that can be acknowledged and recognized by the sitter."

"Like my patient who liked to read the newspaper?"

"Yes, and once the evidential is delivered, I give the message."

"Do all mediums work this way?"

"Mediums have various skill sets, training, tools, and abilities. And readings can be affected by so many variables. How the medium is feeling that day, the spirit's energy and the energy fields around them. The planetary energies, the astral plane energies, and the recipient's mood and frame of mind. Each reading offers an array of varying energies and aspects. And speaking of readings, someone else is here who is eager to say hello to you."

"Who is it?"

"It's your mother. You have similar features, but her hair was straight and dark. She shows that she worked at a desk."

"Yes, my mother was a secretary, and she had straight dark hair. I got my curly red locks from Dad."

"Your mother passed after a long illness. I'm hearing it was cancer."

"Yes," Rebecca said.

"Your mother says, she always thought you'd become a nurse. She is showing me a scene from your childhood, and you're putting bandages on your dolls."

"Yes, I was always healing them," Rebecca said with a laugh.

"Your mother says you are a very good nurse. She is proud of what you do, and how much you care for your patients. Her illness is the reason you became a nurse?"

"Yes," she said.

"Your mother is speaking of your sensitive empathic nature. She hopes you will learn to trust and rely more on your instincts in your personal life, too. She watches you at the hospital, and may be one of the energies that you sense."

"Really?"

"Yes, she nods, confirming this. She is showing me a book." I zoomed in for a closer look. "The title is *Second Sight* and is written by Judith Orloff, a psychiatrist and clairvoyant. This should be helpful."

"Okay, thanks," Rebecca said as she made a note.

"A man joins us now. He's your father," I said as he stood behind Rebecca's chair. "He was about six feet tall, with short, dark curly red hair. He wears a uniform, and offers you a purple lollipop."

"My father was a police officer. He'd bring home lollipops for me, and the grape ones were my favorite."

"He died in the line of duty when you were young."

"Yes, I was only eight years old."

"After that it was you and Mom. Your mother never remarried?"

"No," she said.

"Your parents stand side by side and they want me to tell you they are okay. They say to stop feeling guilty."

A vision flashed before me of a moving van. As I pulled back from the image a map appeared with a red line on it. The van traveled the line south, from Minnesota to Florida.

"You've recently moved to Florida," I said, and saw fresh sprouts. It was one of my symbols. "You wanted to make a fresh start."

"Yes," she said.

'Why is she feeling guilty?' I asked the spirits, and received an image.

"You feel guilty at leaving your parents behind when you moved?" I said.

"Yes, I guess I do. It didn't occur to me until after I moved here, that I wouldn't be able to visit them at the cemetery."

"Your mother says to stop the guilt. There's no reason for it. Their spirits are not in the grave, but alive and here with you now. You can sense that, can't you? Spirit lives on after death."

"I want to think it's true, but I have trouble believing it."

"The spiritual realms are all around us. Your parents are as close to you now as when you were in Minnesota. It's understandable to miss them, and you and your mother were especially close after your father died."

"Yes, I miss her so much," she said through her tears.

"Of course you do. And we not only grieve the person, but events we associated with them. We might miss dining or shopping with them, or just picking up the phone to say hello."

"Yes, I miss those things, and more."

"Seek new enjoyment. Don't be disheartened by living in the past. Your parents want you to enjoy your life. They are happy about your move, and are proud of your career. And they tell me you have a wonderful life ahead of you."

Rebecca pulled a handful of tissues from the box on my desk and dried her tears. "Thank you, I hope I've made the right decision. The hospital staff has been wonderful, and I really like my work. But I'm lonely, I guess, I could use a friend."

An image flashed into my mind, and though I'm usually reluctant to make predictions, I was inspired to tell her this one.

"I see a man wearing a white coat. He is not a doctor, but he does work at the hospital, in a lab or something. You've noticed him, and the way he smiles at you. You know who I'm talking about?"

"Yes, I think so. He asked me to lunch when I first started, but I was too overwhelmed with learning the new job at the time. What about him?"

"Ask him to join you for a cup of coffee."

"I guess I could do that, but why? What do you see?"

"He could be a good friend," I said, though I sensed he'd become more. "I know you miss your parents, but they are okay, so let go of the guilt. You've made a change in your career, and now it's time to focus on your personal life, too."

"Thank you, Jennie. Can I come for another reading sometime?"

"Of course, it would be a pleasure. And ask Megan to put you on our mailing list."

"I'll do that, thank you."

CHAPTER TWELVE

MY AFTERNOON WAS booked with phone consultations, and went by fast. Before I knew it, Deanna was driving us to the workshop.

Deanna parked in front of the familiar old building that housed the classroom where we first met and learned evidential mediumship under Sara Kelsey.

When we entered the room, I caught sight of Sara speaking with one of her students. Seeing her there made me realize how much I missed her and her classes.

After signing in and paying my fee, I waited in line for my turn to say hello. Sara looked radiantly healthy, and her bright blue dress set off her sparkling green eyes.

"How great to see you," she said with a hug.

"You, too," I said, "you look wonderful!"

"You do, too," she said, "and I hear congratulations are in order."

"Yes," I said and showed her my new wedding ring.

"And how are the children and grandchildren?"

"They are doing great," I said and showed her their pictures on my phone. "Evan is three, Lola is four and Emily, is two and about to become a big sister."

"That's wonderful news!"

"Thanks, and how are you?"

"Well, I got a new fella in my life. We've been dating three months."

"Is it serious?"

"I don't know that it's serious, but it sure has been fun," she said, and glanced past my shoulder at the line that had formed. "It's good to see you," she said, then greeted the next person behind me.

I sat next to Deanna, who said, "Teacher's pet."

"What? Why did you say that?"

"Just kidding," she said.

There were so many people streaming in the door that two of the men brought in extra chairs from the storage room.

"This is the largest class attendance I've seen," Deanna said. "Must be over fifty people here."

"Yes, and I only recognize a few."

Sara walked to the podium and brought the class to attention. She introduced herself to the new students, and greeted her returning ones, welcoming everyone. "You may be wondering what spoon bending has to do with mediumship," she said.

"I certainly am," I whispered to Deanna.

"Physical mediumship is the manipulation of energy. Examples include table tipping, levitation, manifesting apports out of thin air, and spoon bending. Demonstration helps shatter the conditioned limiting beliefs we have placed on the material world. It reminds us that there is more than we perceive. More is available to us than what appears as real. Physical mediumship helps stretch us into a higher level of thought."

She held up a tray and said, "As I pass this around, notice the bent spoons and forks on loan to us from previous students. This can be done."

When the tray passed to me, I was amazed by its display of fork tines and spoon handles twisted in spirals and loops, some bent in half. "I hope I can do that," I whispered to Deanna as I passed her the tray.

"How many of you have heard of Jack Houck?" Sara asked. Only a few hands went up. "Jack Houck is an aeronautical and astronautical engineer. And he is famous for his *PK parties* where he demonstrates spoon bending and remote viewing. PK stands for *psychokinesis*, or mind over matter. His PK parties help people, through personal experience, shift beliefs to achieve desired outcomes. PK also serves to explain such things as spontaneous healing, apparitions and materializations."

Sara then played a short clip from the movie, *What the Bleep*. The scene illustrated how space is not empty, and matter is not solid.

When the video ended, Sara held up a spoon and said, "The spoon bends by setting an intention on the physical to see the change we desire. Things happen according to our belief and expectation. It's all about energy.

"See it as already done, as an absolute. As you focus your mind on the area that you intend to bend, a release of thermal energy heats the metal. When it's malleable, the metal might feel sticky or warm. Once in that state, you will only have about thirty-seconds to bend it."

Sara looked at each person in the room, then said, "Believe it, expect it and achieve it. Ask and receive." She pointed at a table at the far wall of the room, and said, "Choose one spoon and one fork, then return to your seat for further instruction."

Deanna and I followed the crowd to the table. I grabbed the utensils at random, and returned to my seat.

"This should be fun," Deanna said as she twirled her fork between her fingers.

I wasn't so sure, and felt a knot of doubt form in my gut. The familiar fear of perfectionism had reared its ugly head.

Once everyone returned to their seats, Sara led us through a guided meditation. Then she said, "Okay, now take the fork and hold the handle between your thumb and index finger. As you hold it in front of you tap into your inner power, focusing on the energy of a past success."

What? A past success? I wasn't prepared for her to say that. My mind went blank, and I couldn't think of one!

"Now holding on to that successful feeling energy," Sara said, "tell the fork to bend. Say it out loud, Bend! Bend! Bend!"

The room became nearly deafening as everyone shouted at their forks. A young girl was the first to jump from her seat and shout, "It bent! I did it!" We all gazed at her fork, its handle impressively twisted.

"Great!" Sara said. "See that, it can be done. Now bring your attention back to the fork you are holding and tell it to bend."

The volume grew louder as everyone shouted at their forks. Soon elated shouts of success could be heard above the din.

I stared at my fork, and shouted, "Bend! Bend! Bend!" But it ignored and mocked me.

Deanna startled me when she jumped from her seat. She did a little dance, then held her fork in front of my face. "Look at this!" she said.

Okay, I'll admit it, I was jealous, which compounded when the guy on the other side of me also showed me his fork's tight loops.

This can't be happening! I took a calming breath, stared at my fork and commanded it to bend. Nothing, nada, zilch.

Sara shouted over the clamor for attention. "Okay, now that you have bent your fork, do the same with the spoon." The classroom renewed its excitement in whoops and hollers. Spoons were bending and twisting all over the room. Students were showing their achievements of twists and bends, and for a few even the bowls had collapsed.

"Once you have bent your spoon," Sara said, "go to the table for another. I brought enough for each student to bend at least three forks and spoons."

As my classmates rushed the table, I remained seated, staring at my fork. Having had no success with it, I picked up the spoon and walked around the room staring at it. "Bend! Bend! Bend!" I commanded. Nothing.

It was time to use force, and I pulled at the metal. But I wasn't strong enough to bend it. I watched my classmates succeed over and over. They were having great fun. Why wouldn't my spoon bend, twist, fold, or morph?

Sara asked everyone to return to their seats. I sank into my chair as she said, "See that? You've proven it to yourself. Anyone can do this."

I held my unbent spoon in front of Deanna's face. She laughed so hard, I had to laugh too.

Sara peered at me. "Bend it now," she said.

I tried, but nothing happened.

"You can do this," she said, "it's already done."

I felt deflated as I tried again with no success.

"Help yourself to the remaining forks and spoons on the table," Sara told the class. "Take them home for practice and have fun with this. Now, let's give some messages. Who wants to go first?"

CHAPTER THIRTEEN

THE ROOM FELL silent as no one volunteered. So Sara selected her first victim, I mean student, and asked him to come to the front of the room.

"I only came here for the spoon bending," he said nervously.

"I know," she said, "you'll do fine." Sara instructed him into his connection with spirit, then said, "Tell us who you see. Is it a man or a woman?"

He blanched, and said, "I don't see anyone."

"Look again, someone is stepping forward."

He peered at the space before him, and took a step back, startled. He looked at Sara and said, "I see a man!"

"Yes, you do. Now how old is he?"

"He's my grandfather's age."

"What is the man doing?"

"He is smiling at me."

"Why is he here?"

"He looks happy. He's celebrating something."

Sara nodded. "You're doing great, now ask for more."

"How do I do that?"

"Ask him for more details. What is his message?"

The student's expression changed; he looked astounded. "I see a wedding!"

"Yes," Sara said, "he is happy about a recent marriage. Who is his message for?"

He looked around the room, then stopped and pointed at me. "His message is for her."

"Thank you," I said, pleased that my father was here acknowledging my nuptials.

Sara thanked the young man who walked elated back to his seat. As always, it was amazing how she connected with what her students received.

She asked for three new volunteers. A woman jumped from her chair, and said, "I'll give it a shot."

Sara welcomed her and two other women to the front of the room. "We are going to do a link message," Sara said. "The first person will describe the spirit; the second will add details, and the third will give the message. Ready?"

The three women nodded in unison. Sara instructed them into spirit, and then asked the first woman, "Who do you see? Is it a man or a woman?"

"I see a woman. She is holding a birthday cake."

"Great," Sara said, and pointed to the next woman. "What can you add?"

"I'm confused. I'm hearing daughter, but I sense she had no children. She was a lonely old woman."

"Don't worry, it'll come together," Sara said, and nodded at the third woman.

"She loved people and enjoys being here with us," she said. "She had no children. Her husband was a minister, and she worked at the church, taking the youths under her wing. The birthday cake is for someone here who had been a member of their church."

Sara looked around the room and asked, "Who can claim this message?"

A woman raised her hand with obvious trepidation. "Tomorrow is my birthday," she said, "and I knew the minister and his wife. But it's sad to hear she was lonesome."

Sara said. "She lived alone after her husband died, but she was not abandoned by her church. The members looked after her."

"Oh, I'm happy to hear that," the woman said.

Sara thanked the three women, and they took their seats. "Now, everyone close your eyes and envision something you want to have happen or achieve. Imagine it in living color, and happening now. Good! It is done! Don't doubt it. Good class, and thank you all for coming!"

As everyone exited the classroom, one woman rushed up to me and said, "I didn't bend anything either."

"You didn't?" I said. "I thought I was the only one."

A man joined us and said, "I didn't bend anything. I don't see the point."

"But I wanted to bend them," I said.

"You ready to go?" Deanna asked, cradling an array of bent utensils.

My shoulders sagged as I said, "I guess so."

☼

As Deanna drove back to my store, I sat pondering my failure. Why hadn't I bent a fork or spoon?

"I'm sorry you're upset," Deanna said. "I had hoped the class would be fun."

"Oh, I'm the one who's sorry, puzzled and embarrassed. I should have been able to do this. I must have some mental block."

"Did you fear failing? Sara says we get what we expect."

"Do you think that's it? But, why? I had looked forward to the class."

"Maybe it's your perfectionist tendency?"

"That could be," I said. "Sara has told me on more than one occasion, that perfectionism blocks my Gifts."

Deanna stopped by my Subaru which was parked in front of the Sunflowers Shoppe. I thanked her for the ride and got out of her car.

"Anytime," she said, "but hey, don't let this get you down."

"I won't," I said, but it already had.

I drove home and carried my pristine utensils along with my low self-esteem into the house. Jake was waiting at the door.

"How did class go?" he asked.

I held up the fork and spoon.

"Aren't they supposed to be bent?" he said.

"Yes, but mine wouldn't."

"They wouldn't? Did anyone else's bend?" he asked.

I nodded, and bit my lip to keep from crying.

"Come here," Jake said and hugged me. "You gonna be okay?"

I shrugged.

"You'll bend them tomorrow," he said, and kissed my forehead. "It's late, you coming to bed?"

"No, I'll be a few minutes," I said. "I want to read up on this. I know it sounds stupid, but I have to figure it out."

"Well, don't stay up all night," he said.

I brewed a cup of tea, and sat at my computer searching, reading and watching videos about spoon bending and PK. It seemed simple enough, but by midnight I still had not bent a thing.

The damn things just wouldn't bend! I held up the spoon for one last try, and said, "I'd love for you to bend. Please bend. Bend! Bend! Bend!" Nope.

Enraged, I tossed the spoon into my purse. I had wanted to do this, and I had failed.

"Screw it!" I said, and turned off the lights as I trudged to the bedroom.

☼

That night I dreamt about spoons. They surrounded, and towered over me as they mocked that I couldn't make them bend.

I shouted at them in my sleep, "You will bend tomorrow!"

CHAPTER FOURTEEN

NOT HAVING ANY appointments until after noon, and being tired from staying up so late last night, I slept in.

Jake had already left for work by the time I got up. I made a green smoothie for breakfast, and sipped it as I searched again about spoon bending.

Time jumped ahead on me, and I had to rush out the door so as not to be late for my first reading. Maybe Kate was right; I did need to set out earlier to arrive on time.

As I drove, I defied the laws of physics, asking my guides to, "Get me there safe and in plenty of time." And they did!

My first appointment was with a Hanna Benson. Why did she look so familiar?

"I was in your store last December, buying a crystal angel for my niece," she said. "You were standing near the counter with a woman who was thanking you for her reading, so I took a card. But I don't know why it's taken me this long to book the appointment."

"Oh, I remember now. I was talking to JD," I said. At the time, I had predicted to Megan that I'd see this person again, and here she was. "What brings you in today?"

"I'm worried about my sister. Can you give me information about her?"

I connected with spirit, and saw a vision of a tall beautiful blonde, sipping a cocktail, swaying inebriated. "Your sister's still with us."

"Yes, that's right," she said.

"She likes to party."

"Yes, she does."

"This is why you're concerned?"

"Yes, I wish she'd take better care of herself, and her child," she said.

An image of a preteen appeared next to the one of the sister. "She has a daughter."

"That's correct."

A man appeared in the vision, and I shivered. "Your sister is dating a fellow who is... how do I say this? He's worse than the ones she usually dates. You really don't want him around her or your niece."

"You must be referring to Eddie."

"Your sister thinks she can handle him, but she can't. He's not the father of your niece?"

"No, Liz, that's my sister, has only been with Eddie a few months."

"This Eddie has a razor edge. She should get away from him. But here's the problem; she's an adult, and you never could tell her what to do. She's your older sister?"

"Yes, we're stepsisters, we have the same mother."

A woman's spirit materialized behind Hanna's chair. "Your mother's spirit is with us now. She's a gentle and loving soul."

"Yes, she was. Liz looks more like Mom than I do, but she doesn't act anything like her."

"Your mother is saying to not judge so harshly. She was a single mother when she met your father. She says she was lucky to find such a good husband. Your parents were very much in love. She says he was the love of her life. She thanks you for looking after him. He lives in an apartment?"

"Yes, in an assisted living facility," she said.

"But she is also showing me a house. You live in her house?"

She nodded. "Yes, I bought my parent's house from them when they moved into the apartment."

"And now you want your father to come live with you?"

"Yes, I do."

"Your mother says he's happy where he is. He has friends there, and enjoys the activities. And the apartment was the last home he had with your mother, so it's comforting to him. He doesn't want to move, or become a burden to you."

"Yes, but..."

"Don't feel guilty, He's happy there, it's a very nice place. And your mother is saying she will come for him when his time comes."

"Okay. Thanks," she said.

An image flashed in my mind, and I cringed. "You are having awful nightmares. It's frightening stuff! I just caught a glimpse."

"Yes," she said, "and the last time I dreamt about that Grim Reaper my mother died. I'm afraid someone else I love is going to die. Is it Liz?"

Unless her sister changed her path, she was headed for catastrophe. "Your niece stays with you?"

"Her name's Suzanne, and yes, she has asked to stay with me every weekend since Liz took up with Eddie."

"Your mother is happy that you are providing a safe haven for her granddaughter. You are a positive influence on her, and Mom thanks you for that."

"Okay, but what about Liz?"

"You've already tried talking to Liz about your concerns."

"Yes, I have."

"She's an adult, and needs to make up her own mind, needs to see things for herself. Rather than approaching her head-on, start dropping subtle hints. Encourage her to get away from this guy without putting her on the defensive. Help her see another way, without making her wrong. Be there for her and her daughter, and pray for her guidance."

"I will, thank you."

☼

After Hanna left I recalled her chilling dreams. Liz could change the future I had glimpsed, and for her and her daughter's sake, I hoped she would before it was too late.

CHAPTER FIFTEEN

MY NEXT APPOINTMENT wasn't due yet, so I took the spoon from my purse and held it. I focused on it as I imagined a ball of energy appear above my head, shoot into my hands and into the metal. "Bend! Bend! Bend!" I said. I heard a giggle, and looked up.

Megan was standing in the doorway laughing at me. "You okay, Jennie?" she said. "Should I be worried?"

I tossed the spoon aside, and said, "I'm fine, what's up?"

"A Mrs. Wilson is here for a reading, but I can't find her name in the appointment book."

"Oh, that's my fault, I took her call while you were at lunch. I must not have entered it."

"Oh, okay, I'll bring her in," Megan said. Moments later she returned with a woman who looked to be in her late sixties. She wore an abundance of rouge, bright red lipstick, brightly bleached spiked hair and a vibrant orange dress. Her whole appearance emitted an aura of neon light.

"Please have a seat, Mrs. Wilson," I said as I pointed to a chair on the other side of the reading table.

"It's Miss Wilson. I've never married. Not that I've lacked suitors, mind you, but none suited me enough," she said as she patted her hair.

"I see. Well, let's get started, shall we?" It took only a moment for a male spirit to appear. He paced back and forth, and it was the first time I've seen a spirit so agitated. I waited for him to settle into one of my symbolic places for father, or grandfather, or uncle, but instead he kept pacing.

"There is a spirit pacing behind your chair. He has dark brown hair, is wearing a tweed jacket with patches at the elbows and is ignoring me."

"That sounds like William. Hello, dear brother," she said, then looked at me in anticipation for the reading to continue.

But I was at a loss for words. I had not gotten anything from this brooding spirit. Since Miss Wilson had already acknowledged him as her brother, I asked him for assistance. *'Why are you pacing? What is your message? Why are you angry?'*

William stopped pacing and looked at me, as if noticing me for the first time. "Where is Andrea?" he said.

"Your brother is asking for an Andrea," I said.

Miss Wilson reddened. "Tell him she couldn't come."

"That's a lie," William said.

"Um, your brother says that's not true."

She shifted uneasily in her seat. "Typical, William, always thinks he knows it all. Guess death hasn't changed that. Tell him his wife gave me her appointment. That's all there is to it," she said. I must have looked confused, for she added, "I am Debra Wilson. It was Andrea Wilson that booked the reading."

William said, "I came here to see my wife. I had impressed upon her the need to communicate. Why has my sister taken her place?"

"William would like to know why you have taken his wife's appointment," I said, curious as well. "And you can address him with your answer. He can see and hear you."

"Right, well, Andrea couldn't come."

"That can't be true!" William said.

"Your brother said that's not true," I said. Jeez, it was uncomfortable being in the midst of their sibling rivalry.

"Look here, William, I am the one here now, so deal with it!"

William looked as surprised as I felt. He said nothing, but started pacing again.

"How can I help you, Debra?" I asked to get the reading moving forward.

Debra smoothed her skirt as she composed herself, and then said, "Ask William where the Deed is. He'll know which one."

William stopped pacing and sent me a vision. "William is showing me a room with a desk, looks to be in a home office. You will find a safe in the floor when you lift the rug. What you are looking for is in there."

"I figured as much, but Andrea said she wasn't aware of any safe. How can a wife not know these things? Now, William, we'll need the combination."

William sent me another block of thought, and I dictated as Debra wrote the numbers down.

"Very good," she said. "We have a buyer for the back two hundred acres and it's a profitable deal for both me and Andrea. Does William agree?"

William nodded.

"He's nodded yes," I said.

"Good, now, William, I have something to say. Andrea plans to marry. She made the appointment to find out about the Deed, but chickened out because she was afraid to tell you about her fiancé. That is why she asked me to come in her place. Think about it, William, how else could I have known about the reading?"

William stopped pacing and sent me another block of thought. "William is not opposed to Andrea remarrying, but he is concerned about the man she has chosen. He has been trying to reach her in her dreams, but she is either ignoring him or forgetting them. You must tell her that he is very concerned. This is why he wanted to speak with her today."

Debra nodded. "I understand and don't see his appeal either. But, Andrea fears if she turns him down, there will never be another man in her life. She doesn't like living alone."

An image of a pasture flashed in my mind, the two hundred acres. "William is concerned the man will take her money when she sells the property. He wants her to be careful."

"Well, first of all, I get half the proceeds. Our parents left it to William and to me. If not for his wife, I'd get it all; but I must honor his will. As for Andrea, I will tell her of William's concerns, but I can't stop her from marrying that man. I'll suggest that she put the funds in a long term investment, perhaps a Certificate of Deposit. If her fiancé doesn't like that, it'll be obvious he's in a hurry to get his hands on it."

That seemed reasonable to me, and William smiled for the first time since the reading began. "Your brother is pleased with that plan," I said.

"That's good to hear," she said.

As William faded from view, someone else materialized by her chair. "Another man in spirit is now with us, and he says, 'Mercy me, what a sight to see!"

"Matthew! Oh, how delightful," she said as her eyes misted with delight. "My goodness, I haven't heard that saying in a long time. It's what he always said to me. Matthew was the only man I ever came close to marrying."

A vision began, and I said, "There was a battlefield, soldiers, gunfire and Matthew dressed in camouflage."

"Yes, he died in battle."

The vision changed, and I watched a much younger Debra walking along the beach with her soldier. I told her about the scene.

"He was so handsome in his dress uniform. He was wearing it the last time I saw him."

"He tried to come home to you. He never thought he wouldn't make it."

Debra nodded as tears fell from her eyes. "We were both young and idealistic. We never considered that we'd not have our wedding." She sighed. "I guess he's the reason I never married. Oh, I've dated some fine men, but no one ever compared to Matthew."

"He says he watches over you."

"I've wondered if he ever came around. Those times he's felt near, I've thought I was imagining it. I've had dreams about him, too!"

Matthew nodded. "He says that's true," I said.

She wiped away her tears and said, "After all these years I'm ashamed at how I must look to him."

"What do you mean?"

"I'm old and wrinkly now, not the girl he dated. He's still young and handsome. Why would he want to follow this old woman around?"

"Matthew's not concerned. A hundred years on Earth is quite different in the spiritual realms. Matthew is connecting with you at the soul level."

"What a lovely thought, thank you. I was beginning to shy away from ever wanting to see him again, you know, when I pass over. When I was younger, I'd think how romantic our reunion would be. But with age I've come to doubt he'd still want to be with me."

"Have no fear of that," I said, "and speaking of age, you have many years ahead of you. Matthew says you took his death very hard. He says that when love comes along, say yes to it."

"Oh, Jennie," she said as she blushed. "I may not have married anyone after Matthew died, but I've not lived life like a nun. I've had many lovers."

"I'm not talking about casual flings and affairs, this is about a romance."

"Romance at my age? You can't be serious."

"But I am."

"Oh? When will I meet this man?"

"I sense you already know him."

"I do? I'll have to reconsider my men to figure this out. How intriguing," she said as a sparkle came into her eyes.

"You already realize who he is, don't you," I said.

She nodded. "But I never wanted to betray Matthew. You're saying he's okay with it?"

"Yes, go for it. You're not betraying him."

"Thank you, how delightful!"

CHAPTER SIXTEEN

MY LAST CLIENT of the day looked tense. As she took her seat, I smiled at her and said, “Welcome, Stacy. How can I help you?”

Stacy nodded at me as she placed a pad of paper on the table, and said, “I have a lot of questions. First, I’d like you to ask my husband, Fred, if I should move back north by the kids.”

“I see, but...”

“Then I need you to ask Jim, my insurance agent, about my policy,” she said.

“Oh?”

“And I want you to ask Lawrence about the air conditioner. It’s not cooling well. I’ve received estimates, but I’m not sure which company to go with.”

“And Lawrence is?”

“Lawrence was my brother, and he always fixed everything around my house. That is until he died last year, rest his soul.”

As Stacy pointed at the next name on her long list, I quickly interrupted her, and said, “Let’s just see who comes in, okay?”

“But I have lots of questions.”

“Yes, but we don’t have the time to answer all of them today.”

She looked dejected as I connected with spirit. A man in spirit materialized next to her chair.

"There is a man standing next to you, holding a large coffee mug in his hand. The mug is white with an image on it," I said as I zoomed in closer. "Oh, the image is a graphic of a brown tree near a blue lake. He got the mug while on vacation. He says he drank several cups of coffee a day in that mug; it was his favorite."

"My goodness, how could you know Fred had a mug like that? He bought it when we were on vacation in Lake Tahoe. And he did drink too much coffee. I was always nagging at him to drink more water."

"He wants to talk about the day you met. He is showing me a lot of flowers."

She smiled. "Oh, that must be the florist shop where I worked. Fred came in one day to buy a corsage for a girl he had asked to a dance. We started talking and he asked me out. He never did take that other girl on a date."

"Fred is laughing at your list. He says you can make your own decisions."

"I don't know how. I need help," she said.

"He suggests that you start with the easiest one. When you need to make a decision, take a step back from the situation and pay attention to how it feels. That will help you follow your intuition. After making the easy decisions, move on to the harder ones."

"But I don't know about air-conditioning, or if I should move."

"Do you want to move?" I asked. "I sense resistance when you mention it."

"Well, I like my neighbors and there's always something fun to do in our community center. Wednesday night is card games, Thursday is bingo, and Friday is movie night."

"It sounds like you enjoy where you live. Tell me about the move."

"My daughter wants me to move into her house. She lives up north, out in the middle of nowhere. There won't be much to do at her place, but watch TV."

"I don't think you need a medium to tell you how you feel about that. Pay attention to how you feel as you talk about it."

Stacy looked startled. "You mean that's all there is to it?"

"Pretty much," I said.

"I've never made decisions. Growing up, my parents always told me what to do. Then I married Fred. We were married nearly fifty years, and he made all the decisions. So I don't know about a lot of these things."

"Well, there is nothing wrong with asking for price quotes, or referrals. But you need to follow what feels right to you."

"So it's about feelings?"

I nodded. "Yes, it's about noticing gut feelings, hunches, intuition and observing how you feel in your heart. But it's difficult to make any decisions when caught up in our emotions. That is why it helps to take a step back, in the role of observer."

"How do I step back?"

"By becoming present in the moment. One method is to look at the palm of your hand. From this calmer state of mind, you can become the observer."

"You make it sound so easy. What if I need help?"

"Call on your angels or a higher power or Fred. He says he'll help any way he can. He says he's sorry; he didn't do you any favors taking charge all those years. He hopes you'll gain confidence now by making your own decisions."

"I'm not sure I can do it."

"Try this, think of an outcome, imagining you've made your decision. How would it feel?"

She closed her eyes a moment, then looked at me. "I'm reluctant to sell my house. It's been my home for over forty years, and I have many memories there."

"And if you moved away?"

"I'm afraid I'll be lonely."

"The unknown can be confusing and scary. Can you visit your daughter for an extended stay to see what living there would be like?"

"That's an idea," she said.

"If you do decide to move, find a place where you could be active. Perhaps a senior center, or a social club, or being a volunteer somewhere. You don't have to sit in front of the television all day, unless you so choose."

"I never thought of that."

"We often fear what we don't know. Even change for the better, can be scary."

"So if it's feels scary, how do I figure it out?"

Her husband sent me an inspired thought. "Shift out of your head and into your heart. Your heart can guide you. Make it a game. Make a decision from your heart, and observe the outcome. With practice you will gain confidence, and learn how to trust your intuition."

"I guess I could try that," she said.

There was a shimmer at her chest, and I telepathically queried Mica about it.

"She'll be crossing over soon," Mica said, "within the year."

'Is there anything I need to tell her?' I asked the spirit.

"Yes," Fred said, "tell her to be happy."

"Stacy, whatever you decide to do, be joyful," I said. "Enjoy each day as much as you can."

"I'll try," she said.

"Why so sad? What's wrong?" I asked.

"I miss Fred so much, and I liked his making the decisions. But..."

"But what?"

"I can't explain it, but I feel a longing to go home. Not to the house where I live, but to a place I don't know, or can't remember. It's sounds silly, but do you get what I mean?"

An image of a portal like the one in Wanda's room flashed in my mind. "Yes, I do understand. But let me assure you, you're not alone. Fred and others in spirit love and support you."

She smiled. "That's good, it gives me comfort. Please tell Fred that I love and miss him."

"You just told him. You don't need an intermediary. You can talk to him whenever you want."

After Stacy left, I ended my workday thanking the spirits and guides for helping me be of service.

CHAPTER SEVENTEEN

SUNDAY MORNING ARRIVED, and I was enjoying a deep slumber when Jake pulled the quilt off me.

"Time to get up," he said.

I grabbed at the soft, cuddly quilt, and snuggled in.

"Come on, Jen, let's get going."

I glared at him. "Why do I have to get up? Where are we going?"

"We need to get to the course. I don't want to be late for my tee time," he said.

Oh yeah, I had promised to ride in the golf cart with him today.

"Come on, Jen, be with me today."

How could I say no to that? It was nice to be wanted. I tossed the quilt aside, and left my cozy bed.

After showering and getting dressed, I found Jake at the table. I thanked him for making breakfast as I sat down. While we ate, he told me about all the flowers and wildlife we should see on the course.

"Remember to bring your camera," he said.

"Yes, I'm looking forward to taking photos." I used to use my good digital camera all the time, and had been a member of the local photo club. But after I got the new smart phone, I found snapping pictures with it to be more convenient, and put the camera away.

"I packed a cooler with water, lemonade and granola bars. Is there anything else that you'd like to take?" Jake asked as we cleared the table.

"No, I don't think so."

"Bring your hat, it's sunny out there," he said as he grabbed the cooler and headed to the garage.

I pulled a beach hat from the closet, put the strap of the camera bag over my shoulder, and followed him to the Jeep. I slid onto the seat and pulled the camera out of its case. I flipped on the switch and it came to life. It felt good to hold it in my hands again, and snapped pictures of Jake as he drove.

At the golf course, Jake checked in at the pro shop while I stayed outside snapping photos of a cat lounging on a sunny bench. The calico ignored me as she basked in the sunlight with her eyes closed. But her twitching ears told me she was quite aware I was standing there. I closed my eyes and listened for the sounds she might be hearing and became aware of the birds singing and chirping in the branches above us. I looked up and spotted a woodpecker. I zoomed in on him with my lens and captured several shots of his beak hitting the tree. I played with the aperture as I took images of flowers.

One reason I like photography was that in focusing the lens, I was capturing a moment. I was already glad I had come here, and we hadn't driven on the course yet.

A loud piercing sound caused me to look up at a hawk soaring overhead. The bird reminded me of the first reading I had given to Jake from his spirit guide, Red Hawk.

"Are you ready to go?" Jake asked as he exited the pro shop.

"Yes," I said, glancing at the bucket of balls he was carrying. "You expect to lose that many balls today?"

He laughed. "These are practice balls. I like to loosen up before I play," he said. I followed him to a golf cart and slid onto the seat. He backed out of the space, and drove to the Jeep where he placed his clubs and the cooler on the cart, then drove us to the driving range.

"I'll be right back," he said as he selected a few clubs from his bag and walked away carrying the bucket. I followed him and snapped several pictures of him swinging his clubs. After he had emptied the bucket of balls, I followed him back to the cart.

We drove to the first tee. I waited in the cart as he walked up to the white markers, then took a swing. I tried to watch the ball, but lost sight of it as it blended in with the clouds.

"Where did it go?" I asked.

"Over by those trees," he said.

I had to laugh at his answer for there were trees everywhere.

He drove the cart up to the ball and hit it again. The ball landed on the green. "On in two," he said with a smile as I snapped his picture.

He carried his putter to the green, took a stance and tapped the ball. It made a soft plunk sound as it fell in the cup. "Parred it," he said as I took his picture again.

Jake played several more holes, when he said, "You can get out and stretch if you want. Just don't get in front of me during my swing. I don't want to hit you with the club or the ball."

I stepped out of the cart and walked over to a thicket of briars. I peeked in for a closer look, surprised to find a group of daisies at the center. I snapped several photos, zooming in and out with my lens before Jake called me back to the cart.

Near the next tee box was a trio of Sandhill Cranes. Two of them pecked at the ground while the third stood sentry. I was snapping their picture when Jake said, "Did you see that?"

"See what?"

"I got a birdie."

"You hit a bird? Where?"

"No, I didn't hit a bird. I got a birdie," he said.

"What's that?"

"I scored under par."

"Oh, that's a good thing, right?" I asked.

"Yes," he said, and I snapped his picture. Jake laughed. "Are you having fun?"

"Yes, I'm really enjoying my camera," I said.

"I can see that," he said, "but I had hoped you'd take an interest in golf."

Realizing how he felt, I decided to pay more attention to his game. At the next hole I walked on to the green with him, and watched him putt. The ball rimmed the hole but did not drop in until he hit it again.

Jake walked over to me, dropped a ball at my feet, and handed me the putter. "Here, you try it," he said.

I handed him my camera as I grabbed the putter, trying to remember the stance I had learned many years ago. I lined up with the hole and hit the ball, missing it by a wide margin.

"Try again," he said, "only instead of striking at the ball, take an easy swing."

I swung at the ball, and it stopped short of the rim. At least I got it close. "That was fun," I said.

"Try it one more time," he said, "and this time, clear your mind of anything but seeing the ball going into the hole."

I lined up with the hole, and imagined the ball dropping in. I took a breath and as I exhaled I tapped the ball with the putter. It sank in the hole! "That felt good," I said as I handed him his club.

He nodded as he handed me my camera, then said, "And now you're in for a treat." He drove around a high bank of hedges and as we rounded the corner a cascading manmade waterfall surrounded by flowers came into view.

I jumped from the cart as soon as it stopped, and ran up to the waterfall, snapping photos from every angle. When I turned back toward Jake, I noticed the glistening ponds dotting the course. The blue sky, green trees, colorful flowers, and green fairways were an awesome array of color, and I hoped my lens would capture it.

The eighteenth green was surrounded by flowers covered with butterflies. I snapped away, especially delighted by the yellow ones that always reminded me of my mother being near.

As we rode back to the Jeep, I reflected on how much I had enjoyed taking the photos. Perhaps it was time to join another photo club and get back to using my camera.

"Did you enjoy yourself?" Jake asked.

"Oh, yes!"

"Are you open to taking lessons?"

"Yes, I was just thinking... Oh, you mean, golf lessons?"

"Of course, what else would I mean?"

I shrugged and smiled at him. Could I find the time for both golf and photography lessons?

CHAPTER EIGHTEEN

MONDAY MORNING I was uploading photos from my camera to my computer when Megan came into my office, and said, "Joyce Dillon's on the phone. She doesn't have an appointment, but asked if you could fit her in for a reading."

"What time?"

"She said she could be here in twenty minutes."

"Okay, that's fine," I said, and finished transferring the images. I'd sort through them later.

JD and her Uncle Carl have referred numerous clients to me. I first met Carl last fall, on the eve of my store's opening. He had been reluctant to sit with me, but with some persuasion, and the offer of a free reading, he became my first client. And he was so pleased to receive a message from his wife that he, and his niece, became two of my most loyal supporters.

I wonder why JD wants to come in today? I put the camera in its case, closed my roll-top desk, and walked out to the store front to brew a cup of tea.

As I glanced out the front window I saw JD helping an elderly woman cross the street. They stepped on the sidewalk, and I rushed to the front door, holding it open for them.

"Hi, Jennie," JD said as they entered the store. "Thank you for seeing us on such short notice. This is my Aunt Rose."

"Hello, Rose," I said, "it's nice to meet you. Would you like a cup of tea?"

"No, thank you," Rose said.

"I would like some tea," JD said as she seated her aunt in the waiting area, then joined me at the coffee counter. As we waited for our tea to brew, she said, "I hope you can help her."

We glanced over at Rose.

JD said, "She can't hear us from here."

"What's the matter?"

"She won't tell me, but something's been troubling her ever since her last doctor's appointment."

"Well, let's see what we can do for her," I said. We walked up to her aunt, and she smiled at us.

"Let's visit with Jennie in her office, Aunt Rose," JD said as she helped the woman to her feet. We escorted her down the hallway to my office, and took our seats at the reading table.

I closed my eyes, and as soon as I connected, a female spirit appeared behind Rose. "Your mother is here with us, Rose."

Rose looked at JD with surprise. "What did she just say?"

"She said your mother's here."

"That's what I thought she said." Rose looked confused.

"Just listen to her, Auntie Rose," JD said. Rose nodded, and looked back at me.

"Your mother is showing me a child's tea set. She says that she often played tea party with you. There was a small white table where you'd sit together. The teacups were white with small pink roses in the design."

Rose's eyes grew wide with amazement as I spoke.

"Your mother is also showing me a white fluffy dog. It's name begins with a letter S. It sounds like snow something."

Rose's eyes lit up, and she said, "Snowball!"

"I remember your talking about Snowball, Aunt Rose," JD said. "You told me that the dog was always getting into mischief."

"Yes, that's right," Rose said with a laugh. "I haven't thought of that dog in years! She was always in trouble. My mother had been told the dog was fixed. But soon after we got her she gave birth to six puppies."

"Yes, your mother is showing me that you wanted to keep one of the puppies, but your father had said no," I said.

Rose's smile faded as she pulled back and folded her arms across her midriff.

'Why the reaction?' I silently asked.

In reply, Rose's mother sent me a vision. A man was hitting a young girl with a stick. The girl was Rose! She cried as he beat her black and blue. I cringed at the vision.

Mica said, "He hit her often. She fears that after dying he will harm her again."

'How can I help?' I asked the spirit.

Her mother responded, and I said, "Your mother says your father can't abuse you anymore."

Rose's eyes glistened with tears as her lip trembled. "He won't?" she said.

"No," I said. A man dressed in a three piece suit materialized behind Rose. "Your father can't hurt you, nor does he want to. He's had his life review, and he is here now to tell you..."

"No!" she said with alarm, "I don't want him here!"

JD took her aunt's hands, and spoke to her in a soft, soothing tone. "He's in spirit, Aunt Rose, he can't hurt you."

I asked for more information. "Your father was in finance, a banker."

Rose nodded.

"He was well liked in the community, and could be very nice. He'd bring you presents from work, like shiny coins or new pens."

"Yes," she said.

"He was a good provider, but when he drank he'd fly into a blind rage. He'd hit you or your mother, whoever was closest," I said.

Rose shrank further into her seat.

"Your father says, 'I'm sorry, please forgive me, Rosie. I come in peace now, and in the hereafter. Please don't fear me."

Rose didn't respond, so I wasn't sure if she heard the message.

"Did you hear me, Rose? Can you sense his spirit near you?" I said.

She pulled further back into the chair, and said, "I don't want him here!"

"Have no fear, Rose," I said. "His energy is soft, gentle and kind, not mean or scary. When we die we reawaken to a larger dimension of reality. We reunite with our higher self. The person you knew as your father no longer exists. His spirit is now holding the image of his former self only so you can recognize him."

She shrugged.

"Your mother is saying, 'Please don't fear your father. There is nothing here but love for you. I will be waiting for you when your time comes, and so will Ray. You won't be alone."

Rose smiled. "Are you saying I'll see Ray?"

"Yes," I said.

"I'd like that," she said, then turned to JD and said, "I'd like to go home now."

Rose had ended our reading. I watched JD help her aunt to her feet, and we all walked back to the storefront.

"I'd like that cup of tea now," Rose said.

"Sure thing, Aunt Rose," JD said as she helped her into a chair.

JD signaled for me to follow her to the coffee counter. "I've heard stories of how her father had beat her and her mother. When Rose turned seventeen she eloped with a guy named Ray. He was very kind, but he died just a few years after their wedding and she never remarried. I think that, other than Ray, she's always had a deep-seated fear of men, because of her father."

"Yes, and I want to tell you something. During her reading I sensed her time was near. This might be what she discussed with her doctor, and the reason for her melancholy. Can I make a suggestion?"

"By all means," she said.

"If you are with her in her final hours, talk to her about Ray, her mother and Snowball. Avoid mentioning her father. He sends her love, but there's no reason to cause her distress."

"Okay, that's good advice," JD said as she stirred her tea. "And I wanted to thank you for being with Caroline at the hospital. She told me and others how helpful you were."

"Glad I could be of service, and I found the experience fascinating."

"In what way?"

"I saw Griffin come for Wanda, and I saw them go into a portal of light with a luminescent being."

"That is fascinating!" she said. "Can I ask a question?"

"Of course, what is it?"

"What about pets? I guess it's silly to mourn a dog. And I realize that losing a pet is not the same as losing a person..."

"Oh, I wouldn't say that. Some people are very attached to their pets. They can become part of the family. People can develop a connection or bond with a pet that some find hard to comprehend," I said, as an image of my dog, Max, came to mind.

Max had brought much joy into my life. For nine years he had been my confidant and steady companion. Just being in his presence helped lift my emotions. And when he passed away, I mourned him as deeply as any valued friend.

I wiped at the tears that still welled in my eyes from the memory of him. "Why are you asking about pets, JD?"

"A friend's dog recently died, and she can't get over the loss. She is sad, angry, resentful and guilty that he died. What would you say to help my friend feel better?"

"I'd say what someone told me when I lost my beloved dog, Max. Perhaps it will help your friend as well."

"Okay, what is it?"

"Only a fraction of our spirit incarnates on the Earth. The larger part of us is waiting in the spiritual realms, welcoming loved ones home."

"I like that idea."

"I thought you might. The book *Coping with Sorrow on the Loss of Your Pet* written by Moira Anderson Allen also helped me deal with my grief. And a friend had emailed me a link to a poem called, *The Rainbow Bridge.* You can search and find the poem online, and it's about our pets playing in the afterlife while waiting to greet us on the other side. Do you think your friend will find any of this helpful?"

JD pulled a tissue from her pocket, and wiped her tears. "I can assure you it has," she said, "since, as you've probably guessed, that friend is me."

"Yes, I kind of thought so."

"Thank you."

☼

After JD and Rose left, I opened my journal and asked about Max. I've had other pets, but none were as intuitive and loving as that dog. I still missed him, and asked questions as I typed. Where is Max? Do our dogs go to the same place we go when they die?

The answer from Spirit was immediate. "There are different levels of energy, vibration and thought. Humans and their pets don't reside or vibrate at the same level, but they can interact. And, like other spirits, pets can look in on the Earth realm, just as you have seen Max in spirit."

Yes, I typed, I've had glimpses of him. And I have heard his collar jingle, and his soft growl. I have sensed him near me. And after he first passed away, I felt his paw touching my leg. And I've had vivid dreams about him.

"Why do humans doubt their dogs have souls? Just look into their eyes and see their compassion. Max helped people feel joy and love during his lifetime. That had to come from somewhere. And isn't that the highest we can all hope to attain?"

Yes, but I miss him so very much.

"What you long for is the way he helped you feel connected to the presence of unconditional love."

Yes, how can I connect that way now?

"Unconditional love resides inside you. You can tap into it when you love yourself and others. You can experience it when you meditate. And you get a deeper sense of it the more you meditate."

CHAPTER NINETEEN

MY NEXT APPOINTMENT was with Leonard, a new client. He looked older than his forty years, his forehead creased with worry, his eyes sad and tired.

"My wife made this appointment. She thinks you can help me," he said.

From his appearance, it was obvious something was troubling him. "It's nice to meet you, Leonard. Let's see what we can do for you today," I said.

He nodded wearily, yawning as I connected with spirit. A gray haired man stood behind his chair. "Your grandfather is here," I said.

Leonard shrugged, and said, "I guess that's possible." He stared down at his hands while I described the spirit who had joined us.

"He was about five feet, six inches tall, and very tan from spending a lot of time outdoors."

The grandfather sent me a vision, camping in a forest, a tent pitched by a stream, a campfire.

"Your grandfather shows me that he enjoyed hunting, fishing and camping with you. He'd tell you stories as you sat together, and have you guess whether the tales were true. He was quite the storyteller."

Leonard looked surprised. "You've described my mother's father," he said.

His grandfather nodded, confirming this was true. He waved his hand to start a new vision. "He is showing me a beach. He is holding a fishing pole and casting out a line."

As I watched the vision I fell into the rhythm of his casting out, reeling in, casting out and reeling in. I became transfixed, and stood up to mimic the casting motion, flicking my wrist to let out the imaginary line, then reeling it back in.

Falling into the hypnotic pulse of the movement, I was pulled into the vision and my office fell away. I was standing on the shore. I glanced up at the sky and saw birds soaring overhead. I looked out at the water, and watched his grandfather fishing. I heard the surf, and the gulls.

All my senses told me I was actually there! And I wanted to bask in and explore this indescribably delicious realm, but Leonard pulled me from the vision when he asked, "What's going on?"

I sat in my chair wishing I could prolong the experience of this blissful state of awareness, undisturbed. But I couldn't as the spirit sent me a block of thought to interpret for my client.

"Your grandfather has been showing me a vision of him surf casting at the shore. But it's not about fishing, or the beach. It's about how it feels to cast out a line, then reel it in."

"What do you mean?" he asked.

"It's about using movement as a form of meditation, about the feeling of relief. He suggests you get into the rhythm of releasing, like when you fished with him."

His grandfather smiled, happy to get his message delivered to his grandson.

"You have been fretting over something you can't figure out. You've lost sleep, and you're stressed about it."

"Yes, that's true," he said.

"Your grandfather says that you have tried to meditate, but find it hard to quiet your mind being so stressed. He suggests you do something that you enjoy which would create a gap in your thoughts. You can't find a solution when so focused on the problem. It's about finding that feeling of release and letting go that allows space for knowledge to come in." An image of a golf ball flashed in my mind. "Do you golf?"

"I used to," he said.

"The other day I was reminded that I can't play golf accurately if I'm thinking about anything else. Your grandfather encourages you to take up an activity that will shift your focus off your problem. When you let go of it, your answer will come in."

"Can't you just give me the answer?" he asked.

His grandfather shook his head.

"No," I said, "because this is about a process. He is giving you a tool to help you solve this, and other challenges. This isn't the only problem you will ever face. Not being able to calm your mind is like revving a car in neutral. You need to disengage, and stop fretting over the problem. Do something else, like fishing or golf."

"And tennis?" he said.

"Yes, any activity that releases your mind from the problem can allow space for the solution to come forward."

"Now I understand why Grandpa liked to fish so much," he said with a smile. "Please tell him thanks."

"You just did," I said.

CHAPTER TWENTY

IT WAS TIME to update my sessions log. And I find it helpful to study my journal entries for insights, patterns or new symbols I have received. One recent reading was about a past life.

In evidential mediumship we strive to provide evidence to the sitter, which a past life reading can't offer. And researching the details of a past life only confirms historical data. How can anyone prove that they were the person viewed in that lifetime?

Even when I have intuitively known, beyond a doubt, that the person I'm reading for is the one I'm seeing in the past, I can't prove it. So I make no such claims. But if a client specifically requests a past life reading, I'll explain all this, and then give what I get.

Sharon, was a recent client who had asked for a past life reading.

"I'm a very good bookkeeper, but feel compelled to write. But whatever I do write, I keep in a drawer because I fear I won't make money at it. Of course, with it sitting in a drawer, it's guaranteed to fail, right?" she said with a laugh. "A friend suggested that my compulsions and fears were stemming from a past life. Do you think that's possible?"

Sharon sat patiently through my explanation of why this was not evidential mediumship.

"I understand," she said, "and I'm eager to get some answers."

So I started the session posing a question to the spirits. "Why is Sharon so compelled to write?"

A vision of a giant book fell on my desk. It was from the *Akashic Records*. The cover opened, and the pages flipped quickly back in time, then stopped. I looked at the page and told Sharon of the vision I saw there.

"It's the 1600s, and I see a young girl... you... wanting to learn to read and write. But you are told that only boys get educated. There was a strong desire, but you never got a chance to write in that lifetime."

The scene ended, and the book opened to a new page. "We have moved forward in time. In this lifetime, you are living in New York City," I said. "This was long ago, when horses, not automobiles, were the transportation of the day."

The vision was so real; I not only saw the horses but heard their hooves on the cobblestoned streets. "You are a teenager in this scene. It is winter, and you are wearing a heavy winter coat with a scarf covering your head."

The scene advanced. "It is now evening of that day. You are sitting with a pen, writing in your diary. You sit alone up in the attic, tucked away in your secret place. You write there every night, about everything that happened during the day, and how you felt about it."

I smiled as Sharon wrote down nearly every word I said.

"To afford ink, pen and paper, you babysit and do other chores. The scene advances. Your mother sees your ink stained fingers and deems it unfeminine. And she does not like that you spend so much time alone writing. You ignore her, and write anyway."

The scene advanced again. "The vision has moved forward in years. It is another winter and you sit alone in the attic, huddled in a blanket, writing a book. Your mother is yelling up at you from the stairs. She says that you will never make money writing."

Sharon gasped. "My mother says that to me now!"

I nodded, and said, "Your mother also told you that you were getting too old to find a husband."

Sharon laughed. "She must again be my mother in this lifetime!"

The pages flipped forward, and I said, "This is a more recent lifetime. You lived in the Midwest on a farm. You were the oldest child in a large family who had moved there. You worked hard at your chores each day, always eager to spend time at night writing stories. Your parents are worried at having so many mouths to feed. There are eight or more children gathered at a long wooden table, and your grandparents also live there.

"The farm had not reaped as your parents had hoped. In this scene, your father sits puffing his pipe as your mother mends clothes. They are by the fireplace discussing their future, not knowing how they'll survive the winter. Their thoughts turn to you, their eldest daughter. They decide that it's vital you marry and help provide for all of them.

"The timeline moves forward and your parents have arranged for you to marry a widower who lives in town. You are repelled by the older man. You don't like him or the idea of leaving the farm. But you have no choice. You are told it is your obligation to provide for the family. This causes you to despise money."

The scene moved forward again in time. "Your parents visit the house often, always to tell you of some want or need. Your husband is generous with them, just as long as you service him in bed. You find this degrading, and you despise marriage."

Sharon sighed. "I guess that's why I've turned down some rather decent proposals."

"A new scene now, years later. Your siblings have grown, and your grandparents and parents have passed on. But one brother continues to ask for money. You resent him."

"I have a brother now who is always borrowing money that he never pays back," she said. "Was he in that lifetime?"

I scanned the vision. "I sense he is that brother," I said. The pages flipped forward and stopped. "Another lifetime, it's during the Civil War. You lived on a farm and in this scene you are in a floor length dress standing barefoot at the stove. Your brother comes rushing in to tell you that he is home from the War. You are thrilled to see him but notice how gaunt he looks.

"It takes a while, with such limited food and supplies, but in time you mend him back to health. Each day you hope your husband will return, but he never does. Your brother is healthy now and you expect his help with the farm. But he never has time for chores, always some excuse. He takes what he wants and you resent him again."

The pages of the *Akashic Record* book flipped back and forth symbolizing that she and her brother had lived many lifetimes together. Sometimes as spouses, or as parent child, but most lifetimes as siblings. I told her this, then said, "He has been in nearly every incarnation. There's stuck energy between you that's as strong as rope.

"Part of your current financial problems stem from your resentment toward him. At the end of your last lifetime you swore that if you had more time you could have worked it out. The Universe was listening and gave you this opportunity to get free from your Karma with him once and for all. Once you release that block you can both advance spiritually."

"How do we release it?" Sharon asked.

"Be aware when he's pushing your buttons. Your reaction means you have clearing to do. Write in a journal about how you feel, to get it out of your system. And pray for guidance on freeing the Karma. When you are with him, take a step back emotionally. Seek new ways of communicating with him. If he's open to it, tell him about the need to clear the energy. If he is not receptive to that, write a letter to his angels asking for help.

"You must stop reacting. And that includes letting him take advantage of you. Don't expect a repayment if you do hand him money. Stop compounding your resentment. Declare that you are forgiving him across all lifetimes and timelines so you can drop your end of that rope."

"I will, thank you."

"As you can see, our reactions can be caused from below the surface of our conscious mind. But we can choose to stop reacting, even to past life patterns. Decide to create new beliefs, in that it's okay to write for money and marry for love. Becoming aware of patterns empowers us to change our future. Daily meditation will also help you gain insights and guidance."

After Sharon left I asked to view one of my own past lives. I saw a vision of cobblestone streets, horses and carriages again. But this was not New York City, it was London. I was the daughter of a merchant, and my father had betrothed me to a wealthy man in France.

I did not want to marry the man or leave England. But my father forced me into the marriage to unite and profit our family. I was miserable in a loveless union far away from my beloved homeland.

The scene moved forward in time, and I saw that I had tried, but failed miserably at learning French. The husband's family thought me ignorant. I was an outcast and desperately homesick for London, so I stole money from my husband and ran away. The scene advanced, and I was in prison. My husband had accused me of thievery and my father disowned me, deeming me a disgrace to the family. They left me to die there.

Good grief, that was depressing. Was the husband or father now Ben? Guess it didn't matter as I had plenty to forgive and release about him in this lifetime alone.

☼

I kicked off my shoes and stretched out on the sofa, with a cozy afghan Bridgette had crocheted tucked around me. I closed my eyes and within minutes I was dreaming of an illuminated path. I was like Dorothy in the *Wizard of Oz*, but instead of a yellow brick road, I was skipping on moonbeams suspended in outer space.

I stopped to gaze down at the Earth below. The lovely planet was half lit by sunlight and half plunged in darkness. It was an enchanting sight to see, when something caught my attention. I looked up and saw a man walking toward me along the strands of light. As he came closer, I saw that he was my beloved ex-father-in-law, James Malone.

"Pop!" I squealed with delight as I ran up to him.

"Hello, Jennie, it's good to see you," he said. "I heard you like hanging out here, so I thought I'd come say hello. I've also heard that you have a thriving mediumship career. Folks around here are quite pleased to have another channel in which to get their messages to loved ones on Earth."

"Thanks Pop. That's good to hear."

"Yes, Jennie, I'm quite proud of you."

I smiled and thanked him.

"I've been checking in on you and the kids. And I look in on Ben, even if he has no belief in such things. You know for an artist, he sure is closed minded. He got that from his mother. And here you are, a lovely and intelligent woman. I can't believe Ben let you go," he said.

"His loss, I've remarried," I said, showing him my ring.

"Yes, I've been told Jake's a good man who loves and adores you. I'm happy for you."

"Thanks Pop. I've loved you as much as my own father, and I miss you."

"I love you too, my dear girl, and have enjoyed seeing you, but it looks like our visit is over."

"Oh? Why do you say that?" I asked.

"Because it's time for you to wake up," a voice behind me said.

I turned around and gazed up at a tall shimmering entity. "Who are you?" I asked.

"I am one of your guides, and you need to answer your phone," he said as he pressed a fingertip to my forehead.

CHAPTER TWENTY-ONE

MY CELL PHONE was ringing as I awoke. I glanced at the caller ID, it was Ben's wife, Jasmine. She was a Scottish Jamaican beauty, who could have been a model, but instead chose to manage Ben's career.

As much as I hated to admit it, she was good for him. And she was kind to my children and grandchildren. And she had always been civil. But since we rarely saw each other but for family occasions and holidays, it was most unusual to get a call from her.

"Hi, Jasmine, what's up?" I said as I answered the phone.

"Have you heard about Evonne?" she said.

I cringed. My ex-mother-in-law, Evonne, and I had never gotten along. And as much as I worked on forgiveness, she remained a thorn in my psyche. And my resentment compounded when my daughter told me she had named my grandson, Evan, after her.

"Jennie? Are you there?" Jasmine said.

"Oh, sorry, what were you saying?"

"Did you know Evonne's been in the hospital? She went in for one thing, which led to another. She's very ill and her doctor suggested Hospice. Ben had her transferred there this morning."

I recalled Cecilia mentioning Evonne was sick, but I didn't realize she was this ill. Why had neither Kate nor Nathan told me about their grandmother? Had my hard feelings toward her made it difficult for them to talk to me about her, even when she was dying? "Where are you calling from?"

"Ben and I are here in Naples with her. We drove down several days ago. I just thought you should know."

"Yes, thank you for calling me. I better phone Kate and Nathan to see how they are handling it."

I dialed my son's cell number. When he answered I said, "Nathan, I just heard about your grandmother. How are you doing?"

"Well, I'm sad to hear she's dying, but it's not unexpected. I had hoped she would meet our new baby, but, what can you do? I've asked Kate to let me know about the funeral arrangements, but I don't want to leave Bridgette this late in her pregnancy."

"Don't feel obligated to come. You visited your grandmother just recently, didn't you?"

"Yes, and I'm glad I did. I told Kate I'd chip in on flowers, and say my own goodbye to Grandma from here," he said.

"Yes, you can say goodbye from wherever you are. Have no guilt about that."

"I don't, but I would have liked to have been there for Dad and Kate."

I thought of Kate. It had only been a few months since Brad's death, too soon for her to attend another funeral. I realized that if Nathan wasn't going, I'd better be with her. "Don't worry. I'll be with your sister when the time comes," I said.

"Really? You'd go to Grandma's funeral?"

"I'll be there for Kate. Now, while I have you on the phone, how is Bridgette doing?"

"Her health has been good. An easy pregnancy so far, but she's starting to get tired every afternoon. So we've decided she should quit her job and take Emily out of daycare."

An image of my two year old granddaughter flashed into my mind. Her reddish blonde hair, freckled face and dark blue eyes were so like her mothers. "That sounds like a good idea, but she'll have to keep up with a toddler all day."

"That's what I thought, but Bridgette says she'll get to rest when Emily's napping."

"I look forward to seeing you all again. Let me know when Bridgette's going into labor so I can get on the road."

"Is Jake driving to Ohio with you?"

"Yes, and while we are there I hope to show him Stan Hywet Mansion and Amish Country."

"Sounds like a plan. I better get back to work."

"I love and miss you."

"You too Mom, bye."

I wished I could see him more often. Nathan was more than my son. He was my friend, and had always been supportive, always had my back. Even when I opened my store last fall, and his father and sister were against it, Nathan stood up for me. He had said to go for it and that he was proud of me. I looked forward to being with him again.

I phoned my daughter. She didn't answer, so I left her a message, "Kate, I heard about your grandmother. Call me."

Phone calls done for now, my next appointment was due any minute. I walked out to the coffee counter in the waiting area, and as my cup of tea brewed, a young woman entered the store.

She was dressed in a dark paisley blouse with black pants and leather boots. She wore multi-layered bracelets and necklaces, and long dangling earrings. Her black eyeliner was thickly applied, and her long black hair had red highlights. It was a look that only such a slim, youthful beauty could pull off so attractively.

She walked over and said something to Megan, who pointed at me.

Must be my appointment. She walked up to me, held out her hand, smiled and said, "Hi, Jennie, I'm Mackenzie."

She was so vibrant and forthright that I liked her immediately. "Would you like a cup of coffee or tea?" I asked.

"No, thanks," she said as she pulled a bottled water from her bag, "I'm carrying."

I stirred honey into my cup, and said, "Follow me."

When we entered my office she stopped to look around, then took a seat. "I like your store," she said, "I've shopped here several times. But I like your office, too."

"Thank you," I said.

"It always feels so good in your store."

Her remark told me she was empathic. "What brings you in today?"

Her brow furrowed. "Is the guy I'm dating my soul mate? Were we in a past life together?"

To be asked so soon for another past life reading gave me pause. I explained to her about evidential mediumship and past life readings.

She shrugged and said, "I understand."

As the reading began the *Akashic Record* book again fell to my desk. As it opened, the pages flipped back in time, then stopped. I gazed at the page and saw a vision from a scene long ago.

"There is a seaside village with numerous fishing boats and sailing ships. It's a busy harbor town on a large island, perhaps in the West Indies. People are rushing to and from the docks, carrying packages and storing freight. And there are dozens of horses and carts. It is so chaotic and crowded, there must have been a lot of injuries," I said, mesmerized by the scene.

"That sounds interesting," Mackenzie said, "but, was I there?"

"I'm looking," I said and then, just like a hawk in the sky, I soared above the harbor and flew to a quiet cove. I saw clothes piled in a heap on the sand. There was a man and a woman frolicking, naked in the water. I told her this, then said, "They are lovers, but something is amiss."

"Really, what is it?" she asked.

"As the scene advances, he is putting on his uniform and she is stepping into a long dress and wears colorful scarves and a lot of jewelry. They are arguing. She is very upset about something he plans to do."

I zoomed in closer and said, "It's about a wedding. He is betrothed to the daughter of a senior officer. The marriage was arranged, and he feels obligated to go through with it. He turns to walk away, and she grabs around his waist. As he walks, she is dragging behind him, on the sand. She begs him to stop. She can't bear the thought of never seeing him again."

"Does she ever see him again?"

The scene advanced in time. "I don't know for certain, but she marries another man. It's a loveless marriage and she longs for her lover," I said. I looked at Mackenzie who was brooding about something. "What's wrong," I asked.

"It sounds like what's happening to me now. My boyfriend promised to marry me, but I doubt he ever will."

I gazed at her, and said, "There's more to it. Is he married?"

She nodded. "Yes, but I didn't know he was when we met. He waited until I had fallen in love to tell me. To complicate matters, his wife is his boss's daughter."

"Oh? That does sound similar."

"Yeah, and now I think I'm..."

"You think you're pregnant," I said.

"Yes," she said, "this should be a happy time. I had hoped to marry him and have a future together. But I'm having doubts. Will he divorce her to marry me?"

Again with the fortune telling? I asked for assistance. An image of the woman that had been her in the past incarnation at the beach appeared, shook her head no, then disappeared.

"I'm being shown that he will not," I said.

"I guess I got my answer. I have a lot to think about," she said.

I was sorry to see her so upset. "I don't get a sense that he's the same fellow I saw on the beach in your past life."

"No?"

"No, I sense this is more about the situation. A pattern or a life lesson rather than about a soul mate."

"That certainly sheds a new light on things," she said.

"This insight can serve to help you overcome, and finally move on from this cosmic challenge."

"Thanks for the vote of confidence," she said. "I hope I can."

CHAPTER TWENTY-TWO

MY CELL PHONE chimed while I walked with Mackenzie to the storefront. I pulled it from my pocket, surprised to see it was Jasmine again. Two calls in one day? Must be important.

"I'm sorry, Mackenzie, but I have to take this. It was nice meeting you," I said, and rushed back to my office to answer it. "Hi, Jasmine, what's up?"

"Ben needs you here."

"He needs me? Why?"

"To be with him and his mother."

"You do remember that we don't get along? And that they both find my being a medium laughable?"

"Yes, will you come?"

I sighed. Naples was several hours away, and I really didn't think it was my place. But Mica was at my ear, reminding me once again, that my work was in helping others. It's not that I minded helping, but not where or when I wasn't wanted.

'Wouldn't going there be unwise?' I asked my guide.

"No," Mica said.

"Okay Jasmine," I said, "where should I meet you?"

She gave me the information for both the hotel where they were staying and the Hospice. "So you will come?"

"I guess so."

"Oh, thank you, Jennie!"

I phoned Jake to tell him the news.

"I can't take off on such short notice," he said, "but I'll be with you for the funeral. Be careful driving down there, and try not to let Ben upset you."

"I'll try," I said, wishing he was going with me. Not just to keep me company on the long drive, but because he was an effective ally around Ben.

I told Megan about Evonne, and that I was going to Naples. "Will you reschedule my appointments for the next few days?"

"Of course. Do you need me to do anything else?" she asked.

"Just keep the store open while I'm gone."

"Will do, and by the way, we got a call about renting Deanna's office."

Even though she had left months ago, I kept hoping Deanna would come back here to work with me. I liked having my friend and fellow medium working across the hall.

"I'll think about it," I said.

Kate phoned while I was home packing my suitcase. "I can't take off from my new job so soon," she said. "And just so you know, I saw her last weekend, and we had a pleasant visit."

"That's good," I said.

"But I plan to attend Grandma's funeral."

"You can ride to Naples with Jake."

"Okay, I'll call him about it. But I have to say, I'm really surprised that you're going there, Mom. I know you don't like Grandma, and you and Dad don't get along."

"It's true that your grandmother never liked me," I said defensively. "But Jasmine said your father had asked for me to come."

"Are you sure? That doesn't sound like Daddy."

"Well, that's what Jasmine said," I said, equally suspicious.

"Guess your mind's made up then. See you at the funeral."

☼

As I drove south, the long drive gave me time to think about Ben. Could we have had a better marriage if his mother hadn't constantly interfered and criticized me?

She had always deemed me as unworthy of being a Malone. Well, screw her, I'm a Walker now.

Maybe this wasn't such a good idea. Ben and Evonne had done nothing but ridicule me. I should just turn around.

It didn't take long for Mica to chime in, "This trip is not about you."

"Thank you, Mica! Thank you for always reminding me that my work is not about me," I said, and wiped away angry tears.

I took a few deep breaths, and from a calmer state of mind had to admit that, as usual, my faithful guide was right. I needed to rise above my pettiness and put my own feelings aside. For some cosmic reason, Ben and Evonne had crossed my soul's path.

And, like it or not, Kate, Nathan, Evan, Lola, Emily and soon to be born, Oliver connected us. My children and grandchildren could not be who they were without Ben and Evonne's DNA added in.

And maybe, just maybe, my marriage to Ben had made me more appreciative of Jake. Ben and his mother may be a part of my past, but Jake was my future now.

CHAPTER TWENTY-THREE

THE HOSPICE BUILDING had wood floors, decorative walls, alcove ceilings and ornamental lighting. I signed in at the registry, and a volunteer escorted me to Evonne's room.

She left me at the door, and when I opened it, I saw Ben seated next to the bed, holding his mother's hand. Jasmine sat perched on the arm of his chair. Evonne was laying in the bed with her eyes closed.

As I stepped into the room Ben looked surprised to see me, and said, "What the hell are you doing here?"

Nice welcome. I turned to leave as Jasmine jumped to her feet and ran up to me. It then dawned on me. It wasn't Ben, but Jasmine who had wanted me here.

She hugged me, and said, "Thank you for coming, Jennie."

"Why is Jennie here?" Ben asked his wife.

"I asked her to come," she said.

Ben glared at me. "Stay if you want, Jennie, but keep your opinions to yourself."

His words stung, but I held my tongue and swallowed my emotions, just like I always had during our marriage.

'Should I leave?' I asked.

"Stay," Mica said.

My spirit guide's presence calmed me; I wasn't alone. I walked up to the opposite side of the bed, and gazed down at Evonne. She was restless, and breathed with great effort.

"They're giving her morphine," Jasmine said.

As if on cue, a nurse entered the room. Evonne settled down a bit as the woman tended to her. After the nurse left, Evonne turned her head ever so slightly, as if she was listening to someone.

Mica said, "Her guides are here, helping her spirit prepare to leave the body."

I nodded.

Ben noticed. "What's with the nod?"

"Oh, I just wondered if her guides were talking to her," I said.

"This is not about you and your woo-woo crap," Ben said.

"Ben, please be civil," Jasmine said from her perch on his chair.

She couldn't be comfortable sitting like that. And they both looked exhausted. And I wished Jasmine hadn't phoned me, I felt out of place.

"Be still and present for Jasmine," Mica said.

Be still was Mica's way of telling me to not let my ego get in the way.

Jasmine rubbed Ben's shoulder, and said, "Perhaps you should tell your mother it's okay to go."

He shrugged, then said, "It's okay to go, Mom. Go be with Pop."

Ben's mention of his father made me smile. I had always loved my ex-father-in-law. He had been a wonderful man, full of love and fun, and I really missed him. I felt a spirit near the bed and sensed it was Pop waiting to take Evonne home.

'Hi Pop', I said silently.

Evonne stopped breathing, and we all leaned toward her. Was that her last breath? No, it wasn't.

I walked away from the bed, took a seat in a chair by the patio door, and picked up a Hospice pamphlet from the coffee table. I opened it to an interesting article. It was about the physical changes that are nature's way of shutting down the body during the spirit's release.

It advised to speak softly to the dying person, and to not assume they can't hear you because hearing is one of the last senses to go.

Evonne's body twitched under the sheets, and Ben said, "Why won't she go? Is she afraid?"

"I think it's just her body's way of winding down," I said.

Ben glared at me.

I scanned the pamphlet for anything that would be of help to him. "It says here not to restrain her, and to talk to her in a soothing voice," I said.

He loosened his grip on her hand, and said, "What should I talk to her about?"

"Tell her about your childhood," I said. "Remind her of the things you did together. Tell her what she meant to you. Tell her about your career."

"Jennie's right," Jasmine said, and patted his back. "Go ahead, Ben, talk to her."

Ben told Evonne about his childhood memories, trips the family took together, and things that I never knew about him. Like the time he was learning to sail, and he flipped both himself and his instructor into the ocean.

He also told her about recent sales of his paintings and what his art meant to him. And he talked about what she meant to him, and about our grandchildren. He spoke to her for some time.

And Evonne grew quiet as he spoke. But when he stopped, she again became restless. This had not been like the sudden passing of my parents, which had been shocking to me, but quick for them. No, this death was drawn out, and I couldn't help but feel sympathy for Ben.

I looked at Evonne. I had always wished we'd become close, but never were. It wasn't that I hadn't tried. But from the day we met she made it clear that she had wanted Ben to marry another. I was always hurt by how often she would bring that up, even after I had given her grandchildren.

But I needed to stop dwelling on the past. It didn't matter, and I couldn't change it. I had to focus on being of service to Ben and Jasmine.

I walked back to the bed and asked, "When's the last time you ate anything?"

"I'm not leaving my mother, Jennie! You go eat if you're hungry. I promised I'd be with her," he said.

His chivalry should not have surprised me. He always had a strong bond with his mother.

"But what about Jasmine? Doesn't she need food, or fresh air, or a nap?"

Ben looked at his wife.

"I'm okay," she said with a weary smile.

Another nurse came into the room and checked on Evonne.

"How much longer do you think she has?" I asked.

"I was surprised to see her when my shift started, so I really can't say. It's between her and God," she said and left the room.

"I am not leaving her, Jennie," Ben said. "End of discussion!"

"I didn't mean anything by it, Ben, I was just asking," I said.

'Jeez, if I can't talk, why am I here?'

"You are here to offer moral support," Mica said. "It's not about you."

Would my guide ever get tired of reminding me of that? I walked over to the sofa and sat down. I closed my eyes, and took several deep breaths. Then I dropped deep to the inner door within. The door usually opens to a wonderful flower garden.

But this time as I opened the door a wall of water came rushing in at me. I tried to force the door closed, but the water was too strong. Talk about a wave of emotion!

I gave up on the meditation, and rested instead. It had been a long day and a long drive. I was more tired than I realized, and fell into a deep sleep.

I don't know how long I slept, but I dreamt I was with my ex-father-in-law, James Malone.

"It's good to see you again, Jennie," he said.

"Again?"

"Yes," he said. We chatted awhile, then he said, "I'm waiting to take Evonne home. It's nearly time."

"Jennie, it's time," a voice in the dream yelled at me.

I opened my eyes, and sensed an energy shift in the room. As I sat up I saw that Jasmine had fallen asleep in the reclining chair. She must be exhausted.

I walked over to the bed, and stood next to Ben.

He glanced up at me, then perhaps too tired for a sarcastic comment, gazed back at his mother.

Jasmine awoke, perhaps also sensing the energetic shift. Together we stood behind Ben, Jasmine's right hand on his shoulder, her left hand clutching mine. We all gazed down at Evonne, her body now peaceful, her battle nearly over.

A golden and throbbing light appeared above her head. The halo floated toward the ceiling as it grew in size. It then elongated into the outline of a human body. As I watched in awe, her celestial body morphed into her features. It resembled her physical body, but it was free of disfigurement. Her cord snapped, and she released.

Evonne's spirit smiled at her son, and then at Pop who escorted her through the patio door. They strolled across the lawn and stood surrounded by foliage. A cone of light materialized from the sky, encircled them and took them home.

"She's gone," Ben said. He swiveled on the chair, put his arms around Jasmine's waist, and wept into her shirt.

Why had he never been as gentle and loving with me?

I looked back at the lawn and realized that Evonne's release had felt like energetic relief. It was over. And while her passing appeared to be a hard labor to us, for her it may not have been so.

She was with Pop now. And I was again reminded that birth and death are only entry and exit points for our temporary ride on Earth.

CHAPTER TWENTY-FOUR

TWO DAYS LATER, I was elated when Kate and Jake arrived at my hotel suite. Nathan had stayed in Ohio, but sent a large floral arrangement.

At the funeral home, Kate handed the director a DVD she had created of images of Evonne with friends and family set to music. I had scanned the old photo albums years ago, and everyone seemed to be enjoying the compilation on the overhead monitors.

Jake and I sat in the second row behind Kate, Ben and Jasmine. Evonne's body might look to be sleeping in the casket, but her spirit was alive and in attendance. But I dare not tell Ben as he didn't believe in spiritualism. So I remained mute.

But her energy grew so strong, my arms shook. So I acknowledged her presence by silently saying, '*I'm sure you're delighted to find you are alive in spirit, Evonne. But I cannot speak about it to Ben unless he asks. I must honor his beliefs and boundaries, so please respect my situation*'.

I'm certain she wasn't pleased, but the energy eased off.

The minister arrived, and gave an inspiring eulogy. And Ben stood up and shared some memories about his beloved mother.

Evonne had always been rude to me and indifferent to Pop, but devoted to her darling boy. They had been close, and I imagined Ben was sorely missing her now. Fortunately, he had Jasmine, a strong woman, to rely on.

After the service, people stood in line to speak with Ben and Kate. Jake had gone to the restroom, leaving me alone in the vestibule waiting to drive Kate back to the hotel.

"I'm mighty surprised you are here, Jennifer."

I turned around and cringed. "Hello, Cecilia," I said.

"What are you doing here?"

"I'm here for moral support."

"For Ben? He's got a wife."

"No, I'm here for Kate."

She looked over at Kate, and said, "Our Kate has grown into a lovely woman. But where is Nathan?"

"He stayed in Ohio with his very pregnant wife."

"Couldn't come to his own grandmother's funeral?"

"He visited her last month when he was in Florida," I said, feeling cranky and defensive.

"Well that's between him and his grandmother. But there's something I want to discuss with you."

Now what? I braced myself and said, "What is it?"

"You may not be as loony as Evonne said. She could be judgmental and difficult. And, boy, didn't I know it, we were friends since childhood."

"You knew her that long? I assumed you met her after she met Pop."

"No, James met Evonne because of me. I had befriended her when she and her parents moved into our neighborhood. And let me tell you, it wasn't easy growing up with that girl. I prayed my brother wouldn't fall for her, but he was smitten. So for his sake, I tried to get along with her. But it wasn't all bad, we had some fun times."

"Can't say that I did as her daughter-in-law."

"Yes, and that's what I wanted to talk to you about. You and Ben gave her two beautiful grandchildren. That's something no one else gave her, right?"

"Right," I said, "at least none other have come forward."

She waved her hand at my sarcasm. "I realize she's hurt you."

"You do, huh?"

"Yes, well, Ben was her world, and you took him away."

I'd never really thought of it that way, and said so. "She always said she wished he'd married her friend's daughter."

"You mean my friend's daughter?"

I shrugged. "I don't know who she was."

"Her name was Vicki, and she was my friend's daughter. She and Ben were good friends; but they never dated. I told Evonne this numerous times, but she tuned it out. Even Ben told her that he and Vicki had no interest in each other. I doubt they would have ever been romantically linked, regardless of you."

It surprised me to learn that the daughter-in-law Evonne had wished for had no interest in Ben, or he in her. "Evonne seemed to like Jasmine," I said.

"Well, for one thing, Jasmine's not as sensitive as you are, so Evonne couldn't push her buttons. And by the time Ben met Jasmine, you had already taken him from his home. So Evonne took great delight in telling everyone Jasmine had stolen Ben away from you."

"But that's not true; we were divorced before Ben met her."

"That may be so, but in Evonne's mind Jasmine was her avenger."

"You've got to be kidding! I don't get it. I'm happy my son has married, and has his own family."

She nodded. "Yes, but you're not Evonne."

Jake walked up and stood defensively at my side. "Everything okay?" he asked.

"Yes. Ben's Aunt Cecilia and I have been having an enlightening conversation," I said, then introduced them.

Cecilia said, "I've been rethinking your psychic business, Jennifer."

"What do you mean?"

"Well, let's just say that I used to find the idea of you're talking to ghosts amusing. But seeing Evonne in that casket, and knowing my own time is drawing near, I'm hoping what you say is true."

"In what way?"

"That our spirit lives on."

Evonne's presence was near us, and I said, "Oh, I'm quite certain it does."

"I hope you are right. It was nice to meet you, Jake. Take care, Jennifer."

"You take care, too," I said.

"She seemed nice enough," Jake said.

"Yes, she was the nicest she's ever been to me."

☼

The following day, the weather for the funeral was cool and clear. A slight breeze danced on the flowers at the gravesite. We stood with the other attendees in a half circle behind Ben, Jasmine and Kate, who sat in front of Evonne's coffin.

After the minister ended the ceremony, Kate walked up to one of the arrangements and snapped off a rose. "I'd like to take this with me, is that okay?" she asked.

"Sure, why not?" I said.

A woman I didn't recognize called Kate over to her. Jake and I continued walking toward the parking lot when Ben stopped us. Jake stood defensively with me as I instinctively flinched. What did he want?

"Kate told me that years ago you scanned all those pictures she used in Mother's tribute video," he said. "I never knew you did that, and I wanted to thank you."

His benevolent manner surprised me, and it took a minute to find my voice. “You are welcome, Ben,” I said.

Jasmine, who had been standing next to him, stepped forward and hugged me. “Thank you for being with us at the Hospice, Jennie,” she said as Ben walked away.

We looked at him and I said, “I wish he didn’t hate me so much. What did I ever do but love him?”

“It’s not about you; don’t you realize that by now?”

“What do you mean?”

“It’s something he needs to overcome emotionally,” she said.

“You could be right, but it seems all I ever do is irritate him,” I said.

“Well, we both appreciate your moral support during these trying times.”

“Thank you, Jasmine,” I said, “and speaking of support, Hospice has a support group. If you find Ben is having a difficult time dealing with Evonne’s passing, it may be a good option for him.”

“I’ll look into it,” she said, “and I hope you and I can get together. Let’s plan lunch sometime.”

“I’d like that. Give me a call,” I said.

We hugged again, and then she walked away at a brisk pace to catch up with Ben. Who would have thought one could find a valued friend in an ex-husband’s spouse?

“Ready to go?” Jake asked.

His voice startled me. I had nearly forgotten he was standing behind me. “Yes, I’m ready to go home” I said, as Kate walked past us and opened the passenger door of my Subaru. “I guess she’s riding with me,” I said.

“Looks that way,” he said. “I’ll follow you; be careful.”

We kissed, and I said, “You stay safe, too.”

☼

As I drove home I kept glancing at Jake’s Jeep in my mirror.

"I guess Grandma would have liked her funeral," Kate said.

"Yes, it was a nice turnout. Who were you talking to after the service?"

"Oh, that was Grandma's neighbor. She wanted to tell me that she was sorry about Brad, and now Grandma."

"Did she upset you?"

"No, why?"

"Because of the way you walked to the car afterwards without saying anything."

"Oh, no she didn't mean to upset me, but I guess the funeral brought up memories."

"Do you want to talk about it?"

"No not really; at least not yet."

We drove in silence several miles, when Kate said, "Was Grandma at the funeral?"

"I felt her presence at her wake," I said.

"Why didn't you say anything?" she asked.

"I didn't want to upset your father. He's already testy with me, and my talking about spirits would have unhinged him."

She sighed and said, "I guess you're right, it's all in the timing. Before Brad's death, I didn't want any part of your beliefs, either. Now, I find the idea of spirit living on after death very comforting. If you hear from Grandma, share it with me, okay?"

"Will do," I said, though I didn't really look forward to hearing from Evonne. "I know, Mica, it's not about me," I said.

"Why did you say that?" Kate asked.

"I'm just beating Mica to the punch."

"What do you mean?"

I laughed. "Mica is often quick to remind me that my work is not about me."

"Oh?" she said. "Well, I guess it's good to have someone to keep you on track."

That was certainly a new way of looking at it, and I said, "Yes, thank you for all your help, Mica."

☼

A few nights later, as I was about to drift to sleep, a familiar and distinctive voice called to me from near the foot of the bed.

"Jennie, tell Ben I'm okay."

"He's not open to hearing it from me, Evonne," I said.

Jake sat up on the bed and looked at me. "Are you talking to Evonne in our bedroom?"

"Yes, she was here," I said. "She stopped by to ask me to tell Ben she's okay."

"I don't like the idea of your ex-mother-in-law hanging out in our room."

"Don't worry, she's no longer here. Besides, I believe there's a spiritual code, so she's not watching us take showers or have sex or anything like that."

"Are you sure?"

"Yes, I'm quite certain."

Jake put his arms around me and said, "That's good, because I'm no longer sleepy."

"You're not?"

"No, I'm not. Want to have some fun? That is, if you're sure we are alone."

I pulled off my nightie, and said, "Does this answer your question?"

CHAPTER TWENTY-FIVE

February

JANUARY TURNED INTO February, and every time Jake asked, "What do you want for your birthday?" I'd say, "I don't know."

All my life I've suffered from some kind of weird amnesia. Every Christmas and birthday, I'm unable to think of anything I want until after the event.

"Surprise me," I said.

My husband was not amused. "You're not making this easy," he said.

"I'm not trying to be difficult." Jeez, was I that hard to buy for?

My birthday arrived on a Sunday, along with low humidity, tropical breezes and clear blue skies. It was the type of weather that both Floridians and tourists craved. Jake treated me to a delicious breakfast, and while we ate he said, "Let's drive up to Blue Spring Park."

The Blue Spring Park, situated along the St. John's River, is a designated Manatee Refuge. Since Jake wasn't working this weekend, and my store was closed on Sundays, we had the whole day to ourselves.

"That's a good idea," I said, "since the weather's too nice to stay indoors."

"Great! You get ready, and I'll pack the cooler," he said.

After changing my clothes, I went in search of my husband. He was in the garage, and I helped him load the camping chairs, a blanket and the cooler into the back of the Jeep.

We were on our way, but as he drove, I wished we had asked Kate and the kids to join us. What's a birthday without family?

"What's wrong?" he asked.

"Oh, I should have planned to see the children today," I said.

Jake smiled at me, and patted my leg. "We'll go see them later," he said.

That elevated my mood. When he pulled into the park, I noticed a picnic pavilion filled with balloons and streamers. "Somebody's having a party," I said as Jake parked the Jeep.

As I opened the door, I heard the distinctive voice of my grandson yell, "Nana's here!"

I jumped from the Jeep, and rushed to Evan and Lola as they ran up to greet me.

Lola asked, "Were you surprised, Nana?"

"Oh, yes I was," I said.

"We kept a secret," Evan said.

"You sure did," I said.

I greeted Kate, Deanna, Megan and Chad, and Ben and Jasmine. If only Nathan, Bridgette and Emily were here, but the distance made seeing them difficult. But I'd not dwell on that today. No, I was going to enjoy my birthday party.

Jake brought our camping chairs and the cooler from the Jeep. I rushed up to help him, and said, "You planned all this?"

"Yes, with Kate and Megan's help," he said. "It's not easy fooling a medium."

"Looks like you succeeded! So is that really our lunch in the cooler?"

"No, its ice and cold drinks. Megan and Chad brought the food I ordered yesterday."

"Thank you, Jake," I said, and kissed him.

Jake and Ben got busy at the grill while I chatted with Megan, Chad, Kate, Deanna and Jasmine. I walked up to the table and lifted the lid on the bakery box to sneak a peek at the cake. It had a large sunflower design. I swiped the icing with my finger and licked it.

"Yum, butter cream, my favorite!"

Lola copied me, licking icing from her finger, too.

After lunch, I held Lola and Evan's hands while we walked on the dock looking at manatees. Two floated side by side, just beneath the surface of the water. No swimmers were in the spring today; the beach was closed during Manatee season. But even if swimming was permitted, the spring's seventy-three degree temperature was too cold for me.

We all hiked the trail to the spring head, called a boil because the water boils or bubbles up to the surface from the aquifer. And we peeked in the windows of the historic Thursby House, built in 1872 and still standing.

When we returned to the pavilion, Jake played cards at a picnic table with Ben, Megan and Chad. Kate sat on a beach mat coloring with Lola. Jasmine was lounging in a chair reading a book. Deanna sat near her trying to bend another spoon. And Evan sat on my lap in my camping chair.

"You want to blow bubbles, Nana?" he asked.

"Sure," I said.

Evan ran over to his mother's tote bag and pulled out the bottle. He ran back and handed it to me. I opened it and blew bubbles that he chased after. I was having fun watching him when a bright yellow butterfly flew up to me.

"Hi, Mom," I said.

"Who are you talking to, Nana?" Evan asked.

I smiled at my grandson. "My mother sends me yellow butterflies to tell me she's near."

"She does? Why? Where is she?" he asked.

"She's in heaven," I said, not knowing what Kate would want me to tell him.

"Oh," he said, "that's where Daddy is. Is your daddy there, too?"

"Yes," I said.

"Is he a butterfly, too?"

"My mother's not a butterfly, she sends me butterflies. And no, my dad doesn't send me butterflies, he sends me geraniums."

"What are gra-nu-mums?" he asked, as he struggled to pronounce the word.

"Geraniums," I said. "They are very pretty flowers, and when I see them I think of my father."

"Why?"

"Because when I was a little girl I helped him plant them in the yard by our house. So seeing the flowers remind me of him and that day."

"Oh," he said. "I like to collect seeds."

"Yes, your mother told me. Why do you do that?"

"Daddy helps me find them."

"That's why you collect seeds?"

He nodded.

That answered that mystery. '*Was he communicating with Brad?*'

"Yes," Mica said.

'*I have to tell Kate about this,*' I said to Mica when a large striped butterfly flew at my cheek.

Evan laughed as he pointed at it, and asked, "Who's that?"

"I don't know. I've never had a butterfly do that before," I said as it circled around and struck my cheek again.

"Maybe it's seeing its reflection in your glasses," Jasmine said, peering at me from over her book.

Why would that be? Almost everyone at the park was wearing sunglasses, and none of them were under attack. But I removed the glasses, and was putting them in my pocket when the butterfly charged me again. This was oddly aggressive behavior for a butterfly.

Evan ran over to his mother and took refuge on her lap. He pointed at me as the butterfly repeatedly darted at my cheek.

"What's with that?" Kate asked, with everyone now looking at me.

"I don't know," I said.

"It's trying to tell you something, Nana," Lola yelled, also finding safety on her mother's lap.

"Ask what it wants," Deanna said.

Curious, I asked Mica, *'What's going on?'*

"It's Evonne," Mica said. "She wants you to tell Ben she's alive and okay."

The butterfly struck my face again. "No, go away," I said, and jumped from my chair and ran around with the butterfly following me. A second butterfly came out of nowhere and deflected the first one.

"Another one?" Kate asked with both her children mesmerized by the sight.

'Who is that one?' I asked Mica.

"Pop," Mica said.

"What's going on over there?" Jake asked.

"Butterflies are attacking Nana," Evan said.

And as weird as it was, I had to laugh at James Malone shielding me from Evonne, just as he had in life.

"Thanks, Pop," I said.

"What did she just say?" Ben asked.

"She said, Pop," Chad said.

"Isn't that just perfect," Ben said, tossing his cards to the table. "Now Jennie thinks my father is a butterfly."

"I doubt she meant that," Jake said.

"Well, that's what she just said," Ben said.

The children jumped from Kate's lap and chased after the butterflies, but they darted too quickly to get caught. Lola laughed as they circled her head, then flew back at my face.

By outward appearances, it looked like fun, but it wasn't. It was most annoying. My ex-mother-in-law was using this tactic to get me to speak up after I had refused.

"We have already been through this, Evonne," I whispered, "I will not say anything to Ben unless he asks. And knowing how he'd likely take it, I don't feel like having him ruin my birthday."

The two butterflies flew off, and Evan said, "Do it again, Nana, do it again. Make them come back!"

"I'm not making them appear, Evan, so I can't make them come back."

CHAPTER TWENTY-SIX

JASMINE ANNOUNCED THAT the butterfly show was over, and it was time for birthday cake and presents. I opened gift cards from Megan and Deanna. Ben and Jasmine gave me a lovely leather bound journal. And Kate and the children gave me amethyst earrings set in a Celtic design.

I thanked each of them for their thoughtful gifts as Jake carried a large wrapped item into the pavilion. He set it on the ground in front of me, and said, "You told me to surprise you, so I did."

It was the largest present I have ever received, other than the bicycle I got in childhood. "What could it be?" I said, as Evan and Lola helped me remove the wrapping.

"What is that?" Evan said.

"It's a golf bag," I said.

"Unsnap the cover, open the zippers," Jake said.

I did so, and found golf clubs, balls, tees, a visor, a glove and a shirt. I gazed at my husband, unsure how to respond.

"All you need is golf shoes," he said. "And I also got you lessons. I do hope you'll learn to enjoy the game, I'd like for you to play with me."

"Thank you, Jake," I said. "I am truly surprised!"

Kate lit the candles on my cake, and everyone sang *Happy Birthday,* with my grandson's voice the loudest and sweetest. He sang with so much heart and enthusiasm, tears of joy came to my eyes.

"Will you help me blow out the candles?" I asked the children.

"Yes," they said, and hopped up on the table.

Evan's eyes were as large as saucers as he looked at the number of lit candles. "How old are you, Nana?"

"Don't ask," I said.

"I like birthday cake," he said.

"I know you do," I said.

We blew out the candles, and Evan clapped as Lola dabbed again at the icing, and licked her finger.

Megan and Jasmine served the cake, which tasted as good as it looked.

After eating, I helped collect and toss the trash into a bin, when the striped butterfly came out of nowhere and hit my cheek.

Everyone stopped what they were doing, and stared at me.

"Okay," Kate said, "this isn't normal."

I looked at Ben, and he took a step back.

"I have to tell you something, so don't get mad," I said.

"Oh, brother, I'm not going to like this," he said.

Jasmine rushed to his side, squeezed his hand and asked, "What is it, Jennie?"

"It's Evonne," I said.

"Are you saying that butterfly is my mother?"

"No, she is not the butterfly."

"That's a relief, you had us worried," Ben said.

"But your mother is using it to annoy me."

"Even if she could do that, why would she?" he said.

"Because I have a message for you that I have not delivered. She's wanted me to tell you since the funeral, but I didn't think you would listen."

"That's probably true, so don't tell me now," he said.

"Now, just a minute," Jake said. "If Jennie has a message, why not hear what she has to say?"

Ben glared at him, then at me. "All right, lady psychic, let's have it. This should be entertaining."

Kate grabbed her children's hands and led them to the dock to look for manatees. Once they were out of range of any outbursts, I stood before Ben.

I felt that familiar lump rise up in my throat, as it always had when Ben's intimidation caused me to swallow my words. But I was tired of retreating, especially on my birthday. If I couldn't speak up today, when could I?

And it wasn't my responsibility that Ben accept the message; it was only my job to deliver it. Spirit works in mysterious ways, so maybe this was a gift, an opportunity to gain more confidence.

And being surrounded by Jake and my friends made this the opportune time to go for it. Yes, today was the day to finally stand up to my bully. Goosebumps ran along my arms, a sign that this was true.

"Ben," I said, "your mother is okay."

"She is, is she? And how would you know that?"

"Because she asked me to tell you," I said.

"She did? Don't you mean the little butterfly told you?" he asked.

"Ben, stop it," Jasmine said.

"Evonne is not the butterfly," I said. "She is using the butterfly to get my attention."

"Why would she come to you? She never even liked you," he said.

His words stung. "Thanks for reminding me and everyone here of that," I said. "But she isn't here for me, she's here for you."

"So my mother speaks to you from beyond the grave? Is that it?"

"Yes," I said.

"Well, if she really lives on and has a message for me, she should just talk to me."

"Maybe she is, but you're not listening. All I know is that she wants me to tell you she's okay. Take it or leave it, I'm not going to argue with you."

"Like I said, it's been entertaining," Ben said, and grabbed his wife's hand. "Let's go."

Jasmine pulled free from his grasp, ran up to me and whispered, "I'm proud of you for standing up to him. At last, and on your birthday."

"Thanks," I said.

"You know," she said, "I think I've been sensing Evonne around our house, but I was afraid to tell him."

I nodded. "Maybe someday he'll be open to it."

Ben was halfway to his car, when he stopped and yelled back at Jasmine, "Let's go!"

Evan and Lola ran up to us as Ben drove away. "Grandpa didn't say goodbye," Evan said.

I hoped they hadn't witnessed his anger. I never want to upset my grandchildren.

Kate hugged her son, and said, "Grandpa had to go home."

"But Grandpa said he'd feed the fish with me," Evan said.

"Some other time," Kate said. "Come help me color in your book."

My grandson kicked at the ground with his shoe, stuffed his hands into his pockets, and pouted as he followed his mother to her beach mat.

Jake hugged me, and asked, "Are you okay?"

I shrugged. "It's the same old story. I guess Ben and I will always have friction. But at least today I stood up to him. I'm tired of swallowing my words, so yeah, I'm okay."

"I'm glad to hear that," Jake said. He hugged me again, then pointed at Evan and said, "You mind if I take him to feed the fish?"

"I'd be delighted," I said.

He walked over to my grandson and said, "Come on, Evan, I'll take you."

Evan leapt to his feet, and grabbed Jake's hand. I watched as they walked together toward the dock, and found one more reason to love that man.

☼

Jake drove us home from the picnic. After we unpacked the Jeep, I said, "Thank you for a great birthday."

"You are most welcome. I guess we all surprised you."

"Yes, you sure did."

"I'm glad you had a good time, but I'm sorry Ben upset you."

"Well, you know what they say, problems present opportunity for growth. I was given another chance to stand up to him, and this time I took it."

"I'm proud of you, and I love you," he said with a kiss. "It's late, you coming to bed?"

"Not yet, I'd like to meditate first."

"Okay, good night," he said.

"Sweet dreams," I said. We kissed again, and he went to the bedroom.

I've always liked the notion that we can tap into extra power on our birthday. It was a good time for making wishes, and I wished to dissolve any anger or resentment toward Ben.

I sat down, closed my eyes and imagined cords dissolving between us. I chanted "OM" as I meditated, and realized that it sounded like home. Mimicking Dorothy in the *Wizard of Oz*, I chanted, "There's no place like OM."

And the homesickness that had lingered in the back of my mind since my astral experience during Wanda's transition, fell away. It was meditation rather than ruby slippers, that brought me home, into the blissful state of love and peace we can all find within.

CHAPTER TWENTY-SEVEN

THE NEXT MORNING, I stopped at the mall on my way to work. As I was leaving, I stepped onto the escalator and saw a vision. It was a sea of energy, and strands of light were everywhere. The filament connected me to the other shoppers and them to each other.

A warmth filled my abdomen, and I looked down at a ball of energy pulsating within me. What was going on? Was I hallucinating? Was this an alternate reality? Had I created this, the mall and the other people?

As I stepped off the escalator the vision cleared. But I felt oddly buoyant, like a cork floating on the current as I walked to the parking lot.

When I slid onto the seat of my car, my sensations returned to normal. I sat a moment and pondered the experience. It had been eerie, yet playful; lucid and ambiguous. Why had I experienced this vision? I couldn't hold on to it long enough to examine it.

"Was this a game? Was life a game? And if so, what is the object of the game?"

"To awaken within the game," Mica said.

"Please, tell me more," I said, but Mica made no further comment as I drove to the Sunflowers Shoppe.

☼

When I arrived at my store, I nodded a quick hello to Megan, and rushed to my office. I opened my computer journal and started typing. I wanted to record all that I had experienced at the mall. But I found it challenging to put into words, so I decided to try intuitive writing instead.

As I typed, I asked aloud, "Is life a game?"

The response was, "Yes and no."

This was not Mica's energy. "Yes and no? What does that mean?" I asked.

"Yes, life is like a game played using Natural Laws to express and create in the physical experience. You attract what you think about when aligned with your feeling and intention vibration. The Soul creates in the direction of your focus. But your soul is only a fraction of the larger part of you. Your Higher Self is vaster than your human mind can comprehend.

"And no, you are not making everyone else up. Each person is also a spiritual being, a fraction of their higher self as well. In other words, you are not making up your husband, he is playing at the Game of Life, too. And you are all connected to the vast unified field or sea of energy you witnessed at the mall. And your game is affected by not only your individual thoughts and emotions, but by the race-mind. This mind is the sum of every living person's thoughts and emotions."

I read what I received, and asked, "If life is a game, what is the object of the game?"

"To awaken within the game. It is an exciting and creative adventure. All who come to interact in the playing field of the Game on Earth have a reason why and how they want to play. Some come into the flesh to enjoy sensations, such as the sunlight, rain and wind on their skin. To experience the tangible. Some come for relationships, to play sports, to travel, to contemplate, to build, create and procreate. Some come to overcome patterns, obstacles, challenges and difficulties. Most come for a combination of reasons. Regardless, life is more about being than doing. It's awakening, becoming your authentic self."

We Earthlings seem to face a myriad of challenges, and I asked, "Is this Game of Life some kind of reality show? Are we spiritual entertainment?"

"It's more for mankind's entertainment. Do you like the beach?"

"Yes, I do."

"What do you like about it?"

"I like to feel the sand, the sun and the breeze on my skin. I like to hear the surf, the birds and children laughing. I like to see the sky, the water and the horizon. It's all good there."

"Yes, and the beach is not the only such place. The entire planet offers the experience of enjoyment."

"Then why don't we?"

"The race-mind clings to fear; but it is evolving."

"Why can't we just be woken up?"

"That would go against the prime directive. Interference would rob mankind of the pleasure of unfoldment."

"How do I play this Game?"

"Realize that you attract what you expect, using your thoughts and emotions. Guard your thoughts and be aware of your emotions. Don't allow your mind to dwell on what you do not want. It's not uncommon for a person to spend ten minutes contemplating what he wants, then spend the rest of the day saying it's not attainable.

"And don't fall into fear. When you get a fearful thought, say something like, 'I no longer choose that'. Let it drop away and replace it with what you do want to think.

"And decide to have fun and enjoy life. Use your emotions like a guidance system to alert you when you are dwelling on fear instead of faith. Believe, or pretend to, that life is for you. Assume that you are always guided to the best outcome.

"Take it day by day, and observe what happens when you drop your fears, pretenses and judgments. What you think and feel equates to what you experience. Play life as a game, and notice what shows up."

"Thank you," I said, and read what I had written. As always the spirit's message was wise and loving. And it revealed how much easier life could be.

I logged off my computer, and noticed the spoon on my desk. What underlying beliefs kept me from bending it?

CHAPTER TWENTY-EIGHT

MEGAN STEPPED INTO my office, and asked, "You okay, Jennie?"

I swiveled in my chair to look at her. "Yes, why do you ask?"

"Because of the way you rushed in here this morning."

"Oh, I wanted to type something before I forgot it." Megan looked radiantly happy, and I said, "What's up?"

"Did you enjoy your birthday party?"

"Yes, I was quite surprised by it. And I was happy to see Chad with you. Have you made up?"

"Yes, we had a long talk and decided to hold off on moving in together until after the wedding."

"He proposed?" I asked as I jumped to my feet.

She blushed, extending her hand. "Yes, last night."

I hugged her, then looked at her ring. "It's a lovely ring."

"It is, isn't it? He picked it out, and I really like it."

"Congratulations! Have you set a date?"

"Not yet, but I've always wanted a fall wedding."

"Don't delay planning it. Ben and I decided ours at the last minute, and it was difficult to find a hall to rent, and get the invitations mailed out. All our planning was stressful and rushed."

"Good advice, and I'll talk to Chad about it," she said. The wind chimes pealed out over the front door. Megan glanced down the hall, and said, "Looks like your next appointment's here."

She left to get the new client and returned within minutes with a Lisa Wells.

We made brief introductions as Lisa took her seat and said, "I'm eager to get started."

"Yes, and spirit is too, for there is a female spirit already with us. She appears to be in her early twenties," I said as I described what I saw. "She had curly blonde hair and is wearing a white apron over her long dress. And she wears a wedding band."

A vision of a map appeared and I zoomed in. "She lived a very long time ago, on a farm in the Northeast. She is showing me a corral of horses, her cabin home, and a large garden she was quite proud of."

I held out my hand, and made a sweep of the invisible alphabet before me. "Her name began with the letter A, followed by a G, then another A," I said. As I felt for the energy of the next letter, the name popped into my head. "Her name was Agatha," I said.

"She is now showing me a vision. She is sitting in a rocking chair by the fireplace. She holds her baby girl on her lap, and her two older children, a son and a daughter, sit on the floor next to her. They are laughing at a story she is telling them. Her smile hides her anger at someone."

I asked the spirit for more information. "She was upset with her husband. But why?" I asked as I zoomed in and out of the scene to gain more perspective.

Lisa leaned toward me with anticipation.

"Oh, I see," I said, "he was very vocal about politics, and didn't care what others thought. Agatha wished he would use caution. She feared retaliation from those who opposed him. In this scene at the fireplace, her husband is out at a political event."

The scene moved forward, and I said, "Agatha is tucking the older children in for the night. She puts the baby in a bassinet in her bedroom, then she falls asleep on her bed. She wakes up coughing, gasping for air. Her room is full of smoke!" I said and coughed due to clairsentience. It took a moment for the sensation to pass.

"Agatha picks up her baby as she calls out to her other children. The smoke filled air makes it difficult to speak. She rushes toward the fireplace, but it's not the source of the smoke. The walls and ceiling are in flames!"

Agatha paused the scene to give me a message, which I repeated. "Agatha says that the fire was set deliberately!"

"Yes," Lisa said, "that's what I was always told."

The scene continued. "Agatha tries desperately to get to her children, but the roof has caved in, and her passage to their room is blocked. She runs outside and around to the back of the cabin, but it's ablaze. The heat singes her hair and reddens her cheeks.

"She shields the infant from the heat as she calls to the children. There is no reply. Frantic, she runs to the front yard and screams for help, but the closest neighbor is miles away.

"It's snowing now as her home becomes engulfed by flames. She shivers in her thin nightgown, and hugs the baby to her. When she realizes the infant is dead, she falls to her knees. She is overcome with grief," I said, pushing through the emotions of the saddest vision I have ever seen.

"Agatha is lying on the ground, gasping for breath from smoke inhalation. With her heart broken, she just lets go. Her spirit releases from the body that's dying in the snow."

Lisa dabbed at her tears, and said, "It's always so sad to hear she died with the baby in her arms."

Agatha's spirit moved and stood behind Lisa. But how could she be one of her grandmothers? "Agatha is showing me that she is one of your great grandmothers, but that's not possible when all of her children perished in that fire."

Lisa started to say something, but I stopped her. "Wait a minute," I said, "there's more to the vision. There is a boy standing next to the cabin. It's her son, he lived!"

Lisa smiled and nodded.

"He runs from behind the cabin, and finds his mother and baby sister dead. He sobs as he hugs them."

"Yes," Lisa said, "that boy was Simon, my great-great-grandfather. I've been told that, unbeknownst to his parents, he would sneak out of his room at night to catch frogs or bugs or whatever. He was in the forest behind their home that evening when he saw two men ride up on horseback and torch the roof. He became instrumental in bringing those men to trial. They claimed they were told the place was empty, which was no excuse for what they did."

"Yes," I said. "Simon is showing me that he had seen the men from the woods. After they rode off, he ran back to the cabin, but he couldn't get to his sister."

Simon's spirit came forward with a message. "Simon wants me to tell you that his sister's spirit slipped free from the body before the flames reached it. Her soul did not suffer."

"That's comforting," Lisa said. "The idea of her suffering that way has always bothered me."

"Yes, it is my understanding that the spirit can release prior to physical death," I said. The scene resumed, and I continued my narration. "Simon's father found him later that night. He was still on the ground hugging his mother, shivering from shock and exposure. It was a miracle he survived."

"I've been told he was a stubborn and determined man," she said.

The scene closed. Agatha and her young son's spirit stood beside Lisa, then Simon aged before my eyes. "Simon is showing me that he lived to old age. Agatha is happy to be reunited in spirit with all her children. She and Simon say that they are grateful to have this visit with you."

"Thank you," Lisa said. "You told their story exactly as I've always heard it from my family."

Agatha sent me a block of thought, and I said, "Agatha says that out of such a horrible event, my son created a legacy."

"She is referring to our family's mission of fighting injustice," Lisa said. "It started with Simon. After tracking down the men responsible for the fire, he became a police officer; as did his descendants. My grandfather became a lawyer, and my father worked for the District Attorney. I planned on law, but chose the police force instead."

"And the tradition continues," I said.

"Yes, my one son is a policeman, the other is a private detective, and my daughter is in law school. Simon's legacy endures. I doubt his mother could have foreseen the good that came from her loss that day."

Simon faded from view, but Agatha remained. Why had Lisa received a message from such distant relatives? Other than the restatement of family lore, I could not offer any evidence. It's unlikely Lisa had even seen a photograph of them. And it's improbable she'd hold any ill-will or animosity toward them. So why was Agatha still here?

The usual reason for most of my readings had been to help the client release grief, sorrow, fear and resentment. So what was the need for this reading? Had it just been to validate the details of the tragedy?

There had to be more, for Agatha was still with us. In my experience, once a message is delivered the spirit leaves. So what more did Agatha have to say?

I acknowledged her spirit, and she sent me a block of thought. "Agatha says that she finds your career interesting. She often follows you while you work."

Lisa laughed. "Sometimes it feels like someone's looking over my shoulder. Must be her."

"She says yes, but sometimes it's one of your grandfathers, or your father."

Lisa stiffened at the comment. I had hit a nerve.

"Why would my father be around?" she said.

A man materialized and stood behind Lisa, in my symbolic location for father. Was he the real reason for this reading?

He nodded and sent me a message. "Your father says he loves you very much."

Lisa laughed. "I don't think so. You've got the wrong man there, Jennie."

CHAPTER TWENTY-NINE

UNTIL SOMEONE INVENTS a device like Thomas Edison's conceived *Telephone to the Dead,* mediums will serve as a channel to the spiritual realms.

And while all mediums are psychic, and not all psychics are mediums, not all mediums are alike either.

I have been trained in evidential mediumship to first give a description of the spirit I am seeing, hearing or sensing. This evidence helps my client, known as the sitter, to recognize and acknowledge the spirit in attendance.

As far as my getting it right or wrong, I've been told that even the best mediums get the entire message about eighty-five percent accurately. Why not one-hundred percent? There are several factors.

For one, the messages are filtered through the medium's mind, emotions and beliefs. This can affect interpretation and is why it is so important for the medium to get out of the way and allow the spirit communication. In other words, I must give what I receive without analyzing it. Doubt and fear can kink the spirit connection, while being in a peaceful state of loving service allows expansion and raising the vibration.

Then there's the sitter's expectation. A client expecting to hear from his departed mother may be disappointed when his uncle shows up. It's not that the medium got it wrong, it's just who came in for the reading.

And if a client is told that her grandfather smoked a pipe, she may not be able to verify that until later, when she can look at old family photos, or ask family members.

Symbols are another factor. For example, if I see my grandfather during a reading, does this symbolize a grandfather, my grandfather's name, my grandfather's description, his occupation, or that he smoked a pipe? Another example is seeing a body of water and determining if it's a geographic location or symbolic.

And the energy flow between the medium, the spirits and the sitter affect the reading. If a sitter's arms are crossed in an attempt to stump the medium, she is blocking the energy flow. Also, everyone's energy dips and peaks throughout the day. And we are affected by the energy on the planet. The medium may be tired, have a headache or upset stomach. All this and more can affect a reading.

So in summary, if a client feels that a medium is wrong, it could be due to a variety of causes, including frequencies, beliefs, expectations, symbols, point of view or energy. Or it could be something the sitter doesn't know about the deceased. This is why the medium needs to be well trained in evidential mediumship to better overcome many, if not all, of these challenges.

So when Lisa said, 'You have the wrong man there, Jennie', my training told me otherwise. She may not want to hear from this person, but without a doubt, the spirit standing behind her was her father. What I needed now was enough evidence for Lisa to acknowledge him.

I asked his spirit to help me, and said, "The spirit is standing in my symbolic place for father. He had dark curly hair trimmed short, with a bald spot on the crown of his head. He had a black mustache, bushy sideburns and thick eyebrows. He was husky, but not fat. He is wearing a black suit with a vest under the jacket, and a pocket watch. He says he often took the watch out of his pocket to check the time. The gold watch casing was etched with an image of a deer. The time piece was an heirloom, handed down to him. You now have it."

Lisa blushed. "My goodness, that all sounds like my father, and I do have his watch."

"Then why did you say I had the wrong man?"

"Because my father never said he loved me. He never encouraged or cared about me," she said as she blinked back her tears.

A vision began. A young girl was playing with dolls in her bedroom. I told Lisa what I saw, and added, "You are brushing a doll's hair. Your father walks into your bedroom, his fists tightly clenched. He tries to hold his anger, but yells at you for being late to dinner. You are shaken by his outburst, but you stand up to him and tell him you didn't hear your mother calling you. He stalks out of the room, but the hot energy lingers. It's unsettling."

"Now you've got my father, Jennie," Lisa said. "He was always yelling at me."

"Yes, and you were sensitive to that," I said.

Lisa nodded.

The scene changed. "Your father is now showing me the dinner table later that day. You are seated with your parents and someone else is there. You have a sister?"

"Yes, her name is Beth."

"She is your younger sister?"

"Yes, and she was Daddy's pet. He only said hurtful things to me and my mother, never to her."

"Your father says he is sorry," I said.

Lisa shrugged.

"Your father's rage and behavior has seeded resentment in you." It was so beautifully typical of spirit, her father wanting to alleviate her distress. I was happy to be of service in his quest, and asked him for more details.

"Your father says Beth looked like his mother, but you and your mother looked like her mother."

Lisa looked surprised, and said, "Yes, I guess that's right."

"At the subconscious level you and your mother were visual reminders of the woman he hated. There was bad blood between them. Something to do with money."

"What was it about?" Lisa asked.

"He says your grandmother swindled him!"

"Really?"

"Yes, but he is truly sorry for how he treated you and your mother. It was not your fault. He wants you to know he loved you both dearly, and never meant to hurt you."

"Well, he did hurt me!"

"Yes, he sees that now. His life review has made this and other things quite clear. He is grateful to have this chance to tell you how sorry he is. He loved you very much. A friend of mine has a saying, hurt people hurt people. Your father felt hurt, betrayed by your grandmother. She claimed she had done nothing wrong. She told everyone that your father was mad at her husband, and taking it out on her. She portrayed the innocent victim.

"Your father never believed your grandfather would cheat him. He knew it was her, but he couldn't prove it. This is what enraged him most. She was lying and getting away with it. Unfortunately, life doesn't always have the happy ending portrayed in movies. Your father is showing me a bee with a long stinger and says, 'She stung me good, and professed her innocence till the very end."

"Well, what on Earth did she do to him?" Lisa asked with renewed interest.

"That's a good question," I said. I had been so caught up in the why, I had neglected to ask the what.

"Your mother's father had promised to leave your parents an income producing property. Your parent's counted on it for their retirement. As far as your father was concerned, it was a done deal. It was after your grandfather's funeral that he learned the will had been altered. Your father was certain your grandmother had instigated, or possibly forged the change."

"Why would she do that?" Lisa asked.

"Your father says it's because she never liked or accepted him." Jeez, that sounded familiar as an image of Evonne flashed in my mind.

"Don't go there," Mica said.

I redirected my focus. "Your grandmother didn't equate defrauding your father with cheating her own daughter."

Lisa leaned back in her seat, deep in thought. "I never realized all the family dynamics."

I nodded. "So now you can see there was more to your father. He felt angry and victimized, but did not intend to cause you or your mother distress. He was so caught up in the drama of his emotions, he'd lash out. But he loved you, even when he didn't show it."

Her father's spirit smiled, pleased I had delivered his message. He sent me another block of thought, and I said, "One other thing. He wants you to know he did not love your sister more. He loved you both. You were the victim of his subconscious reactions and he says, 'I wasted years in anger. Don't waste any more of your time dwelling on the past. Know that I love you and I am very proud of you."

As I spoke, the spirits of her father and Agatha faded from view, signaling the message was delivered.

"Thank you, Jennie. I feel like a weight has lifted," Lisa said.

I gave my thanks to the spirits. Delivering their wonderful messages of love and healing is the reason I enjoy what I do.

CHAPTER THIRTY

IT HAD BEEN a busy week, and I had looked forward to sleeping in. But I awoke early with Jake smiling at me.

"What are you so happy about?" I asked.

"We're going to the course today for your golf lesson. Aren't you eager to try your new clubs?"

Was that today? I smiled at him and with feigned enthusiasm said, "Of course, I am."

"Breakfast is ready," he said. "Come on, get up."

I dragged myself from the bed, then showered and dressed. When I joined him at the kitchen table there was a bud vase next to my bowl of oatmeal. His thoughtfulness melted my heart. "Where did you get the rose?"

"I bought it yesterday and hid it in the back of the refrigerator. I hoped you wouldn't find it, I wanted to surprise you."

"Well, you did. Thank you for the rose and for breakfast."

"You are welcome, but eat up. We have to get going, your lesson's at eight. After that we can play nine holes, or eighteen if you want."

I flinched. I had enjoyed taking photographs at the course, but I wasn't sure I wanted to play golf. Years ago Ben and I played a few times, but never got hooked on the game. But Jake was beaming with joy, so how could I refuse? "Sounds like fun," I said.

I cleared the table while Jake loaded the clubs and cooler into the Jeep.

"All you need is your hat," he said.

I grabbed my cell phone and new golf hat, and followed him out to the garage. I eyed the golf bag and hoped I could play good enough.

Jake smiled a lot as he drove. He patted my leg, and said, "Let's have fun."

I smiled, but my stomach was in a knot. Why was I so nervous? It's just a game. But the closer we got to the course the more on edge I felt. My inner perfectionist awakened, eager to discourage me. *You'll look like a fool out there. And you'll disappoint your husband.* My stomach tightened more.

We arrived at the golf course and Jake parked the Jeep. I followed him into the pro shop where he introduced me to Mike, who was managing the counter. Mike and Jake chatted about golf while I browsed the golf clothes and gadgets on sale. As much as Jake liked the game, I could see why he liked working here.

The front door opened, and we all turned to see a woman enter the pro shop. She was stylishly dressed in a short golf skirt and tight shirt. Her slender tan legs ended at slim ankles adorned with cute little pompoms on the short socks in her spotless golf shoes. She wore a visor above her brow, and her long auburn ponytail swayed as she sashayed to the counter.

She was still a sensuous beauty for her age, and she startled the heck out of me when she made a beeline for my husband.

"Jake! How are you?" she asked as she hugged him.

Jake looked genuinely surprised as he worked to free himself from her grip. "Hello, Veronica. I didn't know you were in town."

"I moved back last week. Colorado was okay, but I missed this place... and you."

My ears perked up. She had my full attention as I walked up to Jake.

She batted her velvet lashes as she spoke, focusing her violet eyes only on him. "You want to play with me, Jake?" she asked as she licked her glossy lips, and swiveled her hip flirtatiously at him.

Mike snickered from behind the counter at my husband's discomfort.

Jake put his arm around me and said, "I'd like you to meet Jennie. Jennie this is Veronica."

"Hello," I said.

She ignored me as she kept her gaze on Jake.

"Jennie is my wife," he said.

She looked startled. "You got married?"

"Yes," he said.

"When?" she asked, pouting.

"Last New Year's Eve."

Veronica grabbed my hand and peered at my wedding ring. She released my hand and said, "Well, congratulations, I guess. But we can still play golf, can't we? Just call me, Jake. You still have my number?"

He didn't respond as we watched her turn away, and walk out of the pro shop.

"You still have her number?" I asked Jake, as Mike busied himself behind the counter.

"I might have it, but I haven't called it," he said.

"Why do you have it?"

"I just never got around to deleting it."

"She seemed a little too happy to see you."

He shrugged. "I didn't know she was in town."

"Hmm," I said. "So have you ever played with her?"

"Yes, we were once golf partners."

"Did you play anything else with her?"

"If you're asking if we dated, we did."

"She's very beautiful."

"So are you. Are you jealous?"

"A little bit."

"Why? I married you."

"Did you choose me because she was in Colorado?"

"No, I married you because I love you."

"Good answer," I said. But why would he quit dating a woman as gorgeous as Veronica?

"I'm not the only man she likes to flirt with," he said, reading my mind.

☼

I followed Jake out to a golf cart and he drove us to the Jeep. We loaded our gear and headed to the driving range. The instructor was waiting for me as I carried my bag to the stand.

He was very patient and helpful as we worked with each wood and iron. I remembered some of what I had learned long ago, but I was glad for the refresher.

The lessons had been a good idea. We practiced driving, chipping and putting. And while I was certainly no pro, I was getting comfortable with the game. At the end of my lesson, I thanked the instructor, and walked back to sit with Jake in the cart.

"How was it?" he asked.

"It went well," I said as he drove us to the first tee.

"Remember during my first reading when you told me about my guide, Red Hawk? You told me that he said it's easier to hit a goal that you first see in your mind. You said to envision the green as I swing the club."

"Oh yes, I remember."

Jake parked at the first tee box, and said, "Just relax, don't try to force the ball. Remember what the golf instructor taught you, and what Red Hawk said."

"That's all, huh?" It was a lot to think about as I carried my driver, tee and ball to the tee box. I tensed as I pushed the tee into the ground and balanced the ball on it. I looked down the fairway at the very distant flag. I lined up and hit the ball. It didn't go far, but it went straight.

Jake teed up and his ball went high and long, landing on the edge of the fairway. We played this way for several holes, with his ball landing further, but mine going straighter. In this manner, we'd end up on the green at about the same time.

I soon realized that the more I relaxed, the more I intuitively played, and the further the ball went. In a way, it was not that different from a reading. I had to not over think while staying calm and focused.

On the fifth green, Jake said, "Come here, I want to show you something." I walked up to him and he turned me to face back to the tee box. "See how far you played the ball to get to this green?"

"Yes, that is quite a distance," I said.

"Golf is a challenging sport. It's a mental game, and you're not reacting to a ball coming at you, like in baseball or tennis. You must strike a small stationary ball that needs to travel hundreds of yards to reach a four inch wide hole.

"To reach that goal, you are playing amidst roughs, trees, sand traps, and water and other hazards. And another challenge is choosing the right club for each play. There's a lot to this game, so give yourself credit for getting that ball into the hole."

Jake's pep talk cheered me and I relaxed more. The sixth fairway was short, but the green sat on top of a hill. As I stood at the tee I focused my intention on my ball landing next to the flag. I hit the ball with my driver. It took a hard bounce off a drainage ditch, bounced up and off the flag pole, and stopped next to the hole.

"What a shot!" Jake said.

It was amazing.

At the ninth hole as I was studying the pitch I had a vision. I saw a stream of energy on top of the green, from the hole to my ball. I tapped the ball keeping my putter in line with the stream, and the ball fell into the hole.

"You did it," he said, "and that was a long putt."

"I just followed the stream."

"The what?"

"I imagined a stream of energy coming from the hole to the ball. I tapped the ball along the stream, and it went in."

"What did the stream look like?"

"It looked darker than the grass, and it shimmered in a line along the surface."

During the last nine holes, Jake's and my putting improved, and as long as I focused, my whole game got better. But I was getting tired, and was grateful when we finished the eighteenth hole.

"Did you have fun?" Jake asked.

"Yes, and I now see why you like the game. It offers mental challenges, skill and exercise. And I enjoyed imagining that I was playing with energy."

"I find golf to be a great stress reliever because when you golf, you should only think about golf. It's like a meditation," he said.

"It is a form of meditation," I said.

He nodded, and said, "Well, now you're in for a treat."

"What is it?"

"The nineteenth hole."

"I'm sorry, Jake, but I'm too tired to play any more today."

"No worries, Jen," he said with a smile, "the nineteenth hole is lunch at the clubhouse."

☼

Jake was already sleeping when I slipped into bed that night. I had enjoyed playing golf with him, and was happy we had something we could do together.

I had learned a lot about technique, skill, thoughts and tools to improve my game. And I had enjoyed playing with the energy streams.

I yawned and drifted inward, at the edge of sleep. So if I can play with energy on the golf course, why can't I bend that darn spoon?

CHAPTER THIRTY-ONE

Reflections

THE PATH OF moonbeams were strung out ahead, like lily pads floating on the surface of a pond. It was great fun to dance along the illuminated strands.

I caught sight of the Earth below, half lit by sunlight and half plunged in darkness. I knelt down to gaze at the lovely planet, then continued my journey along the glittering trail.

As I rounded the corner, a flower garden appeared on my right. The flowers were more colorful and fragrant than any I'd seen on Earth. I noticed a cat peeking out at me from under a bed of flowers.

"Come here, kitty," I said.

The black, brown and white tabby came out to greet me. He looked familiar. "Jinx? Is that you?"

He purred as he swirled around and between my legs. I picked him up. Even in my dream, he was a hefty little fella.

"It's nice to see you again, Jinx," I said and hugged him to me.

He purred louder in response. But something got his attention as his ears twitched and he looked away from me. He was listening to something, and then I heard it too. It was someone whistling in the distance. Then I heard his name called, and the cat jumped from my arms and ran away on the path. Must be Griffin calling him.

The cat jumped from my arms and ran away on the path. Griffin must be calling him.

I returned my attention to the flowers, and had knelt for a closer look when I heard, "Hello, Jennie. Come and sit with me."

Who said that? I ran behind a weeping willow tree, and peered out at the garden. Beyond the grassy field a waterfall spilled into a pond. Someone was sitting on the bench facing the pond. Could it really be her?

"Yes, it's me. Come over here," she said as she patted the seat of the bench.

I strolled up to her, and said, "Hello, Evonne."

"Hi, Jennie, it's good to see you," she said, looking up at me.

Her comment was out of character, as the woman had never been happy to see me.

"I put you through a lot," she said, "and I'm truly sorry for how I treated you."

An apology? This was getting weirder by the minute.

"Please, sit with me."

I sat stiffly on the bench, and studied my ex-mother-in-law. She looked translucent and younger, more as she did in her forties.

"I've had my life review," Evonne said as she gazed at the pond. "And it wasn't what I expected."

"Oh?"

"No, I assumed I'd stand before a judge. Instead, I sat with my guides while I viewed and judged the scenes from my life. But that's not the strangest part."

"No? What was?"

"I reviewed scenes from the point of view of the people I mistreated."

"I've heard about that."

"Yes, and it's truly odd to experience events from another's perspective. Especially those times when you thought you were in the right."

"I guess that would be difficult."

"Yes, but you'll never guess what I found most surprising."

"Oh, what was it?"

"A great deal of those scenes involved you."

"Me?"

"Yes," she said, and looked at me. "I had misjudged you. I always thought the worse of you. And I always resented you."

I nodded. "I'm aware of that."

"I'm truly sorry, Jennie. I now understand that you loved my son, and had tried to make your marriage work. And you blessed me with grandchildren. And you went to the Hospice and my funeral. I wouldn't have done that for you. And no one would have blamed you if you hadn't."

"I'm sorry to tell you this, Evonne, but I didn't do it for you. Jasmine said Ben needed me at the Hospice, but it turned out to be for her. And I attended your funeral to be with Kate."

"I understand, and I hold you no ill will," she said. "But speaking of my death, I was astonished to still be alive. I felt energized once I slipped free of my body. And James was there, waiting for me! Together we left that room and walked among the flowers, as if strolling in the park. But the flowers were most vibrant, much like in your lovely garden here. I hope you don't mind my sitting in your garden."

"No, not at all," I said. "And just so you know, I tried to tell Ben you were okay, but he wouldn't listen to me."

"Yes, I'm aware of that. I'm afraid his closed mindedness is my fault. Before James escorted me from the Hospice room, I saw Ben sitting by the bed, filled with grief. How ironic that I'm the one who taught him that death was the end. I raised him to be inflexible in his beliefs, and I couldn't reach him. But if we can be perfectly honest?"

I shrugged. "I guess so."

"Jasmine has been good for Ben. She doesn't put up with any of his bad behavior. And she has masterfully reined in his inflated ego while boosting his career. I'm afraid I pumped up his sense of self so much, that my son lost touch with the kind nature of his soul. I didn't do him any favors raising him that way. And Ben was such a loving child. I hope in time, Jasmine can help him find his sense of compassion again."

Her words should have stung, but they didn't. "I have to agree with you."

She nodded and said, "Yes, you have such a kind soul, Jennie. And it was during my life review that I realized I had played a pretty important role in your life."

"You did? In what way?"

"As your antagonist I offered numerous opportunities that exposed your insecurities. In pushing your buttons I helped shed light on your life challenges, and what you came to work on in this lifetime. If you hadn't been so insecure, there would have been no buttons for me to push. And that's why I pestered you with that butterfly at Blue Spring Park."

"You were most annoying and persistent. Why did you do that?"

"Because I was challenging you to stand up to Ben. He has always intimidated you. I didn't want him to hold back your Gifts anymore. You need to build your confidence. Stop worrying about other people's opinions. And stop swallowing your words, it's unhealthy and you know it. Speak your Truth, even if you sense the other person doesn't want or understand it. It's not up to you that they accept a message, and it's not for you to judge."

"Are you implying that I've judged Ben?"

"Yes."

"How so?"

"You deemed he wasn't ready to receive my message."

"Well, from the way he reacted I'd say I was correct."

Evonne shook her head. "No, you of all people should realize there's more to us than that. He deflected your words at the conscious level, but it took root in his subconscious."

"It did?"

"Yes, and maybe someday that message will open up to him. But it's not up to you to get him, or anyone else, to accept a message, or to accept you. You get that, don't you?"

"Yes, I guess so."

She smiled at me, and said, "I know you do at Soul level. Again, I'm sorry for how I treated you. I only saw in you what I wanted to see. But now I realize there was more to our relationship than either of us understood. We each played a role we had agreed on before birth. And you pushed my buttons, too."

"Well, as long as we're being honest, you played another role, as a role model."

"In what way?"

"You showed me how not to be a mother-in-law. So I strive to be kind, loving and supportive to my children and their spouses."

She nodded and said, "I had resented that you were not the girl I thought Ben should marry. My son had always been compliant and did as he was told, until your marriage. To me, you were the cause of his disobedience. I hated you for it, but not at soul level. At soul level, there is only love. And it just goes to show."

"Show what?"

"Things aren't always what they seem. Challenges are opportunities for unfoldment. When humans cease having buttons to push, there will be no need for forgiveness with those in the afterlife. If we'd just wake up while in the mortal incarnation, we'd live more from intuitive guidance. When we learn to live more soulfully, we'll experience life at a whole new level. Evolution wise, the realms of earth and spirit could merge as one. It could happen."

"I think I understand what you are saying," I said.

"Well, even if you don't, your soul does. I'm grateful to have this visit with you, Jennie, but I guess it's time," she said as she gazed past my shoulder.

"Time for what?" I asked as I turned around and looked up at a tall shimmering entity standing behind me. "Who are you?"

"I am one of your guides, and it is time for you to wake up," he said as he pressed a fingertip to my forehead.

Moonbeams Poem

I'm dancing in the moonbeams,
Cause its written in the stars,
That the only way to heaven,
Is the Love within my heart.

In the tapestry of our lives,
Spun with light in from the stars,
The great weaver up in heaven,
Wove the fabric that we are.

Let's go dancing in the moonbeams,
Let's weave light among the stars,
Cause the way to be in heaven,
Is to realize who we are.

By, Lynn Seeley Thomas

JENNIE'S STORY CONTINUES

Coming Soon…

Jennie's Gifts Book 3

http://www.LynnThomas.info/Jennie

FROM THE AUTHOR

Thank you for reading JENNIE GIFTS. I hope you have enjoyed it. If so, please take a moment to leave a review on Amazon.com, your favorite online retailer, or at http://lynnthomas.info/jennies-gifts-reviews/

And I appreciate hearing from my readers, so you are invited to email me (lynnthomasbooks@gmail.com) or visit my website. And be sure to be among the first to get updates about this Series, other publications and special offers by joining the list at: http://lynnthomas.info/more

Thank you
~ Lynn Thomas

About the Author

Lynn Thomas discovered her passion for writing in childhood while creating songs, poems and short stories with her mother and her paternal grandmother. The nationally published and award winning author enjoys creating inspirational entertainment. And while she writes what she loves, Lynn loves most to write what she lives.

Made in the USA
Charleston, SC
05 January 2015